CONUNDRA

A.E. Currie

Cover designed by Anne Currie

This book is a work of fiction. Names, characters, places, and incidents either are products of the author's imagination or are used fictitiously. Any resemblance to actual persons, living or dead, events, or locales is entirely coincidental.

A.E.Currie
@anne_e_currie
Visit my website at www.annecurrie.com

Printed in the United States of America

First Printing: Aug 2019

ISBN- 9781089112143

To the team: Mum, Dad, Kath, and the Jons.
Many thanks!

Intemperance is naturally punished with diseases; rashness, with mischance; injustice, with violence of enemies; pride, with ruin; cowardice, with oppression; and rebellion, with slaughter

—THOMAS HOBBES

CONTENTS

PROLOGUE

Utopia Six: Pre-Launch Version 378

The tornado suddenly turned and headed in my direction. *Damn!* I thought.

Between me and it, a small forest was on fire. The twister swept through, caught light, and a second later was racing towards me like a fiery juggernaut. I don't mind admitting it was quite intimidating.

My brother materialised beside me.

"Flaming hell!" he yelled in surprise. "Quite literally."

The burning funnel swept away everything in its path, including a schoolyard full of screaming toddlers and a church of terrified parishioners.

Nemo peered at our impending death as it bore down upon us. "That's a nice piece of work. I always say you can never be too over-the-top with a tornado inferno. When do we go live with it?"

"We don't," I replied. "This is supposed to be a Utopia. The new weather control system is not working quite as well as I'd hoped." I paused, "Still, this *is* the last major side effect."

"Details! Sounds like you're practically there. You look like crap by the way."

The last six months had been fairly exhausting.

"What you need," he continued, "is a holiday."

ARRIVAL

Conundra, September 2054

Night had already fallen when I stepped off the train and onto Conundra station. I pulled out a paper map and tried to flick down my suit visor to magnify it before remembering I had no suit here. This was a tech-free city. At least, for visitors.

The platform was busy. Several hundred people had just disembarked and were standing and staring at the place. It looked like a scene from a 1940's war movie, if every evacuee had just arrived from some random point in history. I glanced at the map, which told me I was in the Nostalgia zone. That wasn't my period. I was planning to walk to the Victorian era.

I was glad Nemo had picked an industrial age for my hotel - at least I could wear vaguely normal clothes there. Even so, I'd had to submit my wardrobe to the verisimilitude committee. I glanced down at my outfit: black trousers, white shirt, black leather coat and goggles. *It's not a neoprene suit,* I thought, *but you can't have everything.*

Surrounding me was a group of Roman senators, wrestling with wheelie-suitcases. A porter appeared and quietly relieved them of their anachronistic luggage. I guessed he'd deliver it to their hotel rooms. In private, they could be as out-of-character as they wanted but in public, themes clearly had to be maintained.

Looking about, I reckoned most of the milling visitors were Romans. A toga would have been a much better costume for a sweltering September. *Damn,* I thought.

On the platform, a few others were as overdressed as me. A dozen men wearing trench coats and wide brimmed hats were loitering around with their collars up, smoking cigarettes. I wondered if there was a convention of private detectives in the city - or of retro flashers. Hopefully crime was all they were there to expose.

I wasn't intending to stay long enough in the Nostalgia zone to find out.

I picked up my battered leather suitcase and looked around carefully. The crowd had quickly thinned out as the guests presumably headed to their hotels. I was in no rush. I knew that officially your Conundra storyline didn't start until you'd arrived at your lodgings and got settled in. *If this was my game*, I thought, *I'd say the same thing, then stick a clue in the first five minutes. See who was paying attention.* I turned slowly in a circle, observing everything going on. I was looking for something that seemed wrong. Was there anything out of place?

I watched the train pull away. It left the few remaining new arrivals alone with city residents playing railway workers, guides, or any other part that might be required for the storylines. I gazed across their faces, seeing expressions that were bemused, excited, bored, keen, horrified, tired.

Horrified. I swivelled back to a figure on the far side of the station, close to the other end of the platform. That was what I was looking for. Horror wasn't one of the emotions I would normally expect from a holidaymaker. Although, I didn't go on holiday that often. Perhaps my expectations were unrealistically high.

A young woman had been looking back over her shoulder with an exaggerated expression of fear. She turned her head and hurried towards the station exit. I decided to follow, pushing my way through a crowd of white-robed Romans that had materialised between us. My eyes stayed locked on my target and I tried not to tread on anyone's sandals with my steel-capped boots. *This is one of the many problems with mixing your genres*, I thought. I always tried to avoid it myself.

The person I was attempting to tail had a cloud of brown hair tucked under a headscarf and was wearing a long raincoat that covered her clothing. It was a patent, and poor, attempt at a disguise – she was clearly being deliberately easy to spot.

It suddenly occurred to me I could be muscling in on someone else's story. I looked around and decided I didn't think so. She wasn't dressed as a Roman and none of the other new visitors seemed to be following her – the only people moving around purposefully on the platform were centurions. I reckoned they looked more like security guards than other guests. *Anyway*, I thought, *if I'm intruding on the wrong plotline the*

Conundra systems will untangle it. That must happen all the time.

I moved carefully through the throng towards the woman. She stopped every few minutes and looked behind her in terror. I didn't think she had spotted me yet. *Her act is a bit overdone*, I thought, *but I'll go with it.* This was a rather obvious plot kick-off but I'd seen worse. I shrugged, if I was being honest, I'd written worse.

I emerged from the crowd just as she disappeared out of the station into the unlit streets outside. Still carrying my suitcase I ran after her, bursting through the double doors in time to see her vanish into an alleyway. That clinched it. So far, so stereotyped. I was supposed to infer from her terror she was a lone woman being pursued by an enemy. It was a classic trope. Of course, in real life no one being chased by a villain would dash into a dark dead-end. *You'd have to be an idiot*, I thought, as I sprinted in behind her.

The passageway was narrow and it was almost pitch black in there. I cursed the Victorians for their lack of IR scopes, pulled a box of matches out of my pocket, and lit one. I saw the woman had reached a brick end wall and turned in seemingly genuine panic. She was actually good, I thought – wasted in this clichéd part.

"Who are you?" she whispered, hoarsely.

"A friend." I replied. That was generally the magic key phrase, even though words are cheap and, in reality, I could have been about to punch her out and nick her handbag.

"Please help me!" she cried. "It's all a lie! They're killing people! We have to stop them!"

"I'll do everything I can," I said, getting into the swing of it. "What are these evildoers called and where can I find them?"

"The castle! We have to tell the Warlock before it's too late! We can't trust anyone else!"

The young woman ran back towards me and was still about four feet away when a sharp crack rang out. She theatrically grasped her chest and fell hard onto her knees. *Ouch*, I thought, *I hope they're well-padded under that costume.*

"Leviathan!" she croaked. "Run!"

At that moment, another bullet hit the wall about a foot from me. *That's cutting it close,* I thought, *but I can take a hint.* Recognising my cue to scarper, I ran out of the passage and back onto the street. I took off at speed in the direction of my hotel.

At the end of the road, I stopped and looked back just in time to see a dark figure wearing a distinctive homburg hat slip back into the station.

CONUNDRA

Angelsea, August 2054

Nemo's idea was intriguing. I did need a holiday and I'd been meaning to visit Conundra for years.

Before 2036, Conundra used to be called Colchester and was a small city in the East of England. The town's improbable claim to history was it had once been the capital of Roman Britain. That reign had been ended in AD 61 by Boudicca, a Queen of the local Iceni Celts, when she torched it during her rebellion against the Roman occupation. Colchester never fully recovered and Londinium swiped the title of capital. Having apparently learned no fire prevention lessons, in the apocalyptic Hot Summer of 2036 Colchester was one of the few places in Britain to be utterly destroyed.

To be razed once might be regarded as misfortune; twice looks like carelessness. However, that past was not what made Conundra worthy of my attention.

In 2037, the newly formed state became the only one in Britain to opt out of the Panopticon supernation. Although it recognised WorldGov, visitors to Conundra could not access the all-seeing-eye. In fact, they couldn't use any modern technologies. When the Warlock had rebuilt the place from the literal ashes that was part of his Deal.

Ah, I thought, *the "Warlock's Deal"*. It was this pact between Conundra's sovereign and his subjects that really interested me. I'd wanted to see their society in action with my own eyes for ages because, uniquely in the civilised world, I couldn't view it through the Panopticon.

What was fascinating about the city was all the inhabitants had chosen to be something that, to Nemo and me, felt like a denizen. These Conundrans seemed to have as little control over their lives as chatbots in one of our VR game worlds.

Like us, the folk of Conundra were constantly observed. Unlike Panopticon citizens, the subjects of Conundra had no access to the data on themselves or anyone else. They were watched and manipulated but they were blind. The residents and visitors couldn't talk to Deus or access the net. In fact, they had no technology at all developed after 1955.

That July, Nemo and I had contracted Omniscience Industries to run all of our critical systems and, for the first time in over a decade, I could take myself offline for more than a few minutes. Now my brother had organized me a vacation where I'd be cut off for a whole week! My first holiday in, *err*, I thought, *ever?* It would be great.

BAR

Conundra, September 2054

Two hours after my train pulled into Conundra, I was sitting in the main bar of Fogg's Hotel with a Scotch, a new notebook, and a sharp pencil on the table in front of me. The last two I'd found in a complimentary basket in my room.

I picked up the pencil and jotted down everything I remembered of the victim's words before her dramatic death.

Mysterious Victim:
"Lies and killing people" - A conspiracy?
"The Castle" - The place?
"Find the Warlock" - The person?
"Trust no one" - Of course not, the usual.
"Leviathan" - What's that?

Other Comments:

Was the Homburg-wearer related to the shooting?
Is the victim actually dead? Or just wounded?

I underlined the victim's last words a few times: 'Leviathan' was clearly a vital clue. Was it the name of a secret organisation? Perhaps a person – the ring-leader? This was fun. I could see why Nemo suggested Conundra for a vacation. Of course, the whole thing was appallingly clichéd, but I was impressed by how fast the plot had got moving. They weren't wasting any of my holiday time.

I smoothed my map out and took a gulp of my whisky. The whole city was roughly circular and only a few miles across with a river snaking through it. The station I had arrived at was on the northern edge in the Nostalgia zone. I circled it – my story had started there. The Victorian sector I was currently in was located in the north east. Around the western side were the large Medieval and Elizabethan zones as well as some more niche interests. The middle of the city, inside the restored city wall, was the biggest and most popular sector: Roman. In the centre of that lay Castle Conundrum – the home of the Warlock.

After my encounter with our first victim, my obvious next step would be to check out the castle. I sighed. I hated to be so predictable or to get into the story funnel immediately. Once you'd stepped into that, you might not notice much of anything else until you were spat out at the reveal. No, normally whenever I visited a new virtual reality world my first move was to chat with the local denizens and explore. I liked to get a feel for the place before I started chasing down any one thread. My gut told me to treat Conundra no differently from VR. I decided I wouldn't run after the first clue I'd been given.

I also had an ulterior motive for my visit to Conundra beyond just playing whatever game they'd assigned me - entertaining as that might be. Blindly following their storyboard wouldn't help me achieve my larger aim.

I was savouring my drink and pondering my plans for the following day when the chair next to me scraped back and a surprisingly good-looking man sat down. He appeared to be about thirty and was wearing a green velvet frock coat.

"Mind if I join you?" he asked with a smile.

"Please do. Nice jacket by the way," I replied. "I'm Lee. Are you a guest or a local?"

"'Paul, I'm a guest – just arrived. This is my first time here. I'm really looking forward to whatever they've got lined up."

"What did you ask for?"

"Mystery and romance. How about you?"

"My brother organised it for me as a surprise. He seems to have gone for a deadly conspiracy." I grinned, "It's already started. It's good so far – very relaxing."

"I like the idea of investigating something, but I've no idea how to approach it. I've never done anything like this before." Paul gave me a charming grin, "The woman behind the bar pointed me at you. She said you'd just arrived as well? Maybe we should team up."

I looked across at the bartender, who waved in a friendly fashion. *Great*, I thought, and wondered how I was going to politely ditch Paul. He seemed perfectly nice but essentially clueless. He obviously didn't know anything about the city yet and was bound to slow me up.

At that moment, an attractive young woman in a white frilly dress plonked herself down at the table with us. I sighed and started to pack away my papers. I could see I wasn't going to get anything useful done for the rest of the evening.

"Hi, I'm Lee," I stretched out my hand to the new arrival. "I'm a guest."

"Yes, I know," she replied.

"Let me guess - you were directed here at the bar?"

I looked over at the barkeeper, who winked. I couldn't make out what that was about.

"My name's Esther. I've just got here too." She looked pensive, "I'm quite nervous to be honest. I don't play a lot of games and this is all rather new to me."

An idea occurred to me. "Esther, meet Paul. You're both here on holiday and neither of you knows where to start, but these games are designed to be fun and straightforward. Why don't you work together? You could start by telling each other everything that's happened since you arrived. Perhaps you'll spot some clues? Let's kick off, how did you both end up here?"

Ten minutes later, with a sense of relief, I left the couple happily discussing their favourite pizza toppings and past vacations. I felt smug about my social engineering. I reckoned they'd have a good holiday together; I could get on with things without any rookies holding me back; and no one would feel slighted and give me a downvote.

I suddenly remembered I didn't have to worry about downvotes here. If I'd wanted to, I could've told Paul and Esther to bugger off and leave me alone - there was no reputational bill to pay for rudeness in Conundra. I wondered how I felt about that. It seemed unthinkable I'd deliberately upset them. They were obviously pleasant and well-meaning, so why would I be obnoxious just because there was no downside? I frowned. If I lived in Conundra full time would that change? Would currently inconceivable behaviour become entirely possible if there were no repercussions for my social scores? I decided I doubted it, not least because either of them could still punch me on the nose - the low-tech version of a downvote.

After bidding a friendly goodnight to Esther and Paul, I strolled past the bar on my way to bed. I smiled to myself as I thought about the next day, wondering if any more innocent victims would be killed in front of me.

As I walked by, the bartender looked startled to see me leave so early and waved me over.

"I couldn't help overhearing part of your conversation," she said. "Did you book this holiday yourself?" I shook my head, "What kind of storyline were you expecting?" she asked.

"My brother booked it," I replied, "it's a murderous conspiracy, which was a good choice on his part - I'm already enjoying myself."

"Actually," said the bartender, looking embarrassed, "it's not. The system has you signed up for a romantic break. Your brother must have wanted you to have some R&R. That's why I pointed those two over to you - just to cover all the bases."

She smiled, "I can absolutely guarantee you won't run into any murders in Conundra."

FOGG

Conundra, September
2054

Before sunrise, I found the same barkeeper laying breakfast tables in an empty dining room. I had resolved to get up early to grill her before the other guests appeared. The night before, I'd been taken aback by her comment - it seemed highly unlikely Nemo had signed me up for a romance. There'd clearly been some mix up with his booking.

The mistake, however, implied that by wandering into that shooting I'd stuck my boot into someone else's storyline. I wasn't too worried I'd spoilt things for the real target - the Conundra systems should notice I wasn't their intended guest and re-stage the scene for the correct person.

Nevertheless, I was annoyed. I'd started to get into that mystery.

I wanted to find out what happened next and had decided to see if I could follow up the leads anyway. Worst case, I reckoned, I'd hit a dead-end. Best case, I might learn something about how the systems here worked behind the scenes - a romance was too simple for what I needed to know.

"You work a long day," I said to the bartender, cheerfully.

"Indeed," she replied, "but we live upstairs so it's not too hard. I always get a few early risers and I like to have everything set up before six."

I started to help her out with the tables. I found being useful was a good way to get denizens to talk.

"How long have you lived in Conundra?"

She peered at the glass in her hand, considering, and then polished it with a tea towel. "I came in '41 - right at the start really. I ran my own cafe back then, when it was just the Romans." She shook her head, "I've never roasted so many dormice."

"Ha!" I snorted, then realised she wasn't joking and turned it into a cough. "The name's Lee, by the way."

"I know," she replied, picked up another glass. "Mine's Fogg. Phyllida Fogg."

I must have looked skeptical.

She laughed, "Almost everyone here takes a nom de guerre, so to speak. I changed my name when I moved to this sector in '48. I qualified for a hotel by then. Now here I am with my own place." She gazed around the dark paneled room with pride.

I looked about appreciatively, "How does it work? Do you just run the hotel or are you part of the games too?"

"Oh, every subject is part of the games. We all get a morning briefing and then more instructions from the council a couple of times a day." She gestured at the cameras around the walls and the flowers on every table, which I'd already spotted contained hidden microphones. "The council keeps a close eye on how things are progressing and tells us what to do next to keep all the stories on track."

It reminded me of the way I managed our Utopia games but this set-up sounded way more personalised and high maintenance.

"Do you ever get involved in a plot yourself?" I asked, curious.

"Of course! That's the whole reason we live in Conundra." She was clearly enthusiastic about the place, "Our lives are interesting and they actually make sense." She waved about her, "I pay my taxes and play my roles and the council provides me with my dream existence. Last year, I solved a murder with a sidekick. That was great, I'd recommend it." She shrugged, "Next time I'll be the sidekick, but that will be fun too." She put down a glass and started folding napkins, "I've also planned and executed a daring bank heist. That's how I got this hotel - we found the deeds in the vault." She smiled, "I met my husband on that job."

I finished setting one table and moved on to the next. "Isn't all that adventure a bit exhausting?"

Fogg chuckled, "Yes it would be. Mostly I leave the adventuring to the guests and live a normal life. I just help the visitors along." She paused and then inquired, "On that front, is there any guidance I can give you?"

"Well, at some point I'm supposed to go to the castle. I've also got to find the Warlock."

Phyllida nodded sagely, "Eventually, everyone visits the castle and meets the Warlock. That usually comes at the end."

I wondered how they got that to work. There were tens of thousands of visitors. The Warlock must get nothing else done. I did a quick calculation: if they scheduled carefully and everyone had one minute with him, that would still leave him no time to eat or sleep. Perhaps they merged multiple stories into a single audience at the end? Or maybe they used canned video? It would be interesting to see what they came up with.

"What should I visit in the city before then?" I asked.

"All the sectors are interesting, but I'd start just down the road at the Enlightenment Coffee House. They always get the best info and the coffee is excellent." She paused, "Although, they are a little eccentric."

I thanked her and put my goggles on, then remembered. "Phyllida," I turned back to ask, "does the name 'Leviathan' mean anything to you?"

She thought for a minute, "It sounds familiar but I can't quite place it," she paused, "I think I may have seen something in the Gothic sector."

The Gothic sector? I thought. *How Bram Stoker.*

BROCHURES

Angelsea, August 2054

Nemo had booked me into a hotel in the Victorian sector.

"Think Steampunk," he'd said. "I've got you some goggles for your outfit," he grinned, "you'll like them."

I picked up one of their glossy brochures and flicked through it.

"Come and live your fantasies!" read the cover. "Romance, mystery or thrilling adventure. Enjoy it all – for real!"

No one in the world-building business could fail to be aware of Conundra. No matter how good VR got, it still wasn't reality. The man behind Conundra had famously reckoned he could do better than a virtual world.

No one knew where the Warlock or his cash had come from. He mysteriously appeared in 2037 with his trademark white hair, heavy eyebrows, and silver moustache. He bought up the smoking ruins of Colchester, renamed the place, and immediately started to rebuild.

According to the top rumour amongst game players, the Warlock was a live action role-playing obsessive who'd won the last lottery before the Hot Summer. However he'd come by his money, he seemed happy to spend it. The rebuild happened fast. In 2040, he opened Conundra's first zone, which offered total-immersion Roman mystery holidays. By then, the Warlock had opted out of the Panopticon and excluded our drones, arguing that what happened in Conundra stayed in Conundra.

His premise worked. Visitors were happy to sign away their Panopticon rights for a few days, in exchange for a good story. The LARP city was so successful he decided to expand. He added the Medieval sector next.

Then things changed. In 2041, the Warlock started advertising for subjects.

THE CELT

Conundra, September
2054

The sun was shining and according to the concierge no storms were due that day. I left my coat behind and wandered out into the cobbled street in my shirtsleeves. I pulled my watch out of my waistcoat pocket and glanced at the face. It was seven o'clock in the morning and already sweltering - even in the strong breeze.

In front of the hotel, I found myself standing in a narrow street surrounded by tall, industrial-looking buildings of sooty brick and dark iron. I knew there was no actual industry here and the dirt was just part of the window-dressing. Conundra was a tourist town. However, I approved of the well-executed fakery. In reality, I suspected most of the buildings were restaurants, hotels, theatres and museums. According to my guidebook there was a Watt steam engine around here somewhere that had been rescued from the Hot Summer. I decided I'd look for that later.

I strolled south, passing a lady in a floor length dress and a gentleman in morning suit. They were walking arm in arm. The Victorian gent tipped his top hat at me and I nodded back. On the other side of the street, I watched a Roman centurion struggling to unwrap a choc ice while the horsehair plumes on his helmet blew about wildly.

I had known most visitors hired costumes from the Conundra outfitting operation before they arrived. I hadn't realised until I got here what a big part of the experience dress was. I'd managed to scrape together enough clothes of my own for my costume but now I wished I'd hired something more spectacular. At least, I thought, Nemo's goggles were cool.

I walked into a small park and checked my map. The Enlightenment Coffee House was close by - just over the river. I meandered across an ornate iron footbridge and on the other side saw a well-tanned, muscular man sitting on a park bench finishing a bacon sandwich. He was dressed in a knee-length leather tunic and carrying a huge, double-headed axe.

I stopped. "That looks heavy?"

"Tell me about it," he replied, cramming the end of his breakfast into his mouth, then slowly heaving his weapon onto his shoulder. "I've already lugged this thing halfway across the city. I'm exhausted." He laughed, "You'd think I'd be used to it by now - I work on the Central Belt Irrigation System." He said it proudly, then added thoughtfully, "That's mostly picks though - turns out they're lighter."

He looked pleased with himself for name-dropping his real-world job. It was certainly a high status occupation. The new weather patterns of sun and heavy rain made field irrigation a requirement for most of England. Digging ditches by hand was tough labour, but we all knew it doubled the agricultural yields and, of course, we couldn't use so many machines for it any more.

WorldGov paid well for food productivity projects and they usually recouped the costs with a tax levy on the farms that benefited. The Panopticon also made loads of money from video feed sponsors - their livestream of sweat-covered men driving picks into the earth was hugely popular for some reason.

"Irrigation? That's valuable work! I'm Lee, by the way," I shook his hand, "are you enjoying Conundra?"

"Call me Dave. Yeah, it's good here. I'm a key figure in a violent uprising against the Romans, but I thought I'd nip out and do some shopping." He put down his axe again and grinned disarmingly, "I'm heading to the castle next. I'm told it's worth a look. Come along if you want?"

I thanked him but walked on. I'd leave the Warlock and his castle for later in the week. First, I wanted to do some prep work.

I left the park and continued south on a wide street, keeping my eyes open for a backstreet on the right called Dickens End. I finally spotted it - a tiny, dark alley that couldn't have been more than a few feet wide. I walked carefully down the passage with my shoulders brushing the walls until I came to an almost hidden shopfront. A sign outside read 'The Enlightenment Coffee House'. Peering through the glass, I could just make out dim light. I pushed open the door and went in.

SUBJECTS

Angelsea, August 2054

According to the booklets they'd sent to Nemo, Conundra kept expanding. They added a small tented area for Celts next, which from the photos seemed to be heavily Boudicca-themed. They'd also got into 'experiences'. In my imagination, the Celtic camp experience would be shouting about Romans whilst already blue in the face, but I suspected it'd actually be something boring like pottery and woodcraft. I yawned.

Conundra must have been making good money from their holiday packages because in 2041 the Warlock decided to take it a step further. He chose to introduce permanent residents into the city state. The Warlock's Deal for these new so-called subjects was one of the first and only challenges to the Panopticon's oversight.

Conundra banned all tech, including Panopticon access, for their new populace. In exchange for that loss, the state of Conundra promised to manage the lives of its subjects. It vowed to give them each their own story and provide the excitement, suspense, and resolution that real life seldom delivered.

The Panopticon assemblies objected noisily at first but were silenced by WorldGov. Provided Conundra satisfied its responsibilities to feed and house its inhabitants and to maintain the WorldGov rule of law, President Gates saw no problem with turning off the Panopticon in the new state – provided the subjects were free to change their minds at any time and leave. Very few did.

Conundra joined the old tax havens, North Korea and a handful of other anarchic states in completely opting out of Panopticon society. Unlike those other places, however, Conundra was open for business.

THE COWBOY

Conundra, September 2054

Inside the Enlightenment Coffee House, it was surprisingly shadowy. The room was lit by flickering, domed gaslights on the walls. I wondered how they'd managed that given WorldGov had banned domestic gas well over a decade ago. *A simulation?* In which case, it was an excellent one.

The place was clearly inspired by a classic Victorian library or, if we're being honest, probably a Harry Potter one. Rows of leather-bound books stretched upwards until they disappeared into the gloom. Huge blackened oak ladders reached down out of the dark.

In the middle of the room were four large refectory tables covered with books and maps. The place was empty of customers, apart from one man in a far corner wearing steel-rimmed glasses and a tweed suit. He was poring studiously over a thick tome whilst sipping what appeared to be an oversized latte.

I finally spotted the counter. Standing behind it was a cadaverous-looking cowboy, who tipped his hat courteously at me.

"Morning pardner. What can I getcher?" he said in a plausible Texan drawl.

I walked over, "I'll have a black coffee."

"Coming right up."

He was wearing a tasseled waistcoat in tan suede. Over the edge of the counter I could just make out the tops of his chaps. It was a good costume.

"I'm Lee," I stretched out my hand, "if you don't mind my saying, you seem a little anachronistic."

"Nate McGraw," he replied as he shook, "and cowboys are genuine Victorian. The Wild West began in the 1860's and the whole thing was over by 1900. I'm out of place, maybe, but not out of time." He flicked up his hat and grinned, "No, what I'm taking chronological liberties with is the name of this establishment. The Enlightenment ended a hundred years before Queen Victoria was born. No one ever objects to that. They only baulk at the Stetson." He twirled his hat around his finger, then handed me my drink in a huge mug.

I sipped at the coffee, which was surprisingly good, "Phyllida from Fogg's Hotel sent me down here for information."

"Did she now," he replied. "How can I help?"

"Does the name 'Leviathan' mean anything to you?"

I noticed the customer in the corner stop reading and look up at Nate and me.

"Leviathan? Isn't that Thomas Hobbes? Try the philosophy section. You're a Panopticonner ain't ya?" I nodded, "You'll find him near your guy Kant."

Nate pulled a wooden box out from under the counter and rustled through it before handing me a card. Written on the thick white paper in copperplate handwriting was a short code: 140. I stared blankly at it.

"The Dewey Decimal System for the classification of books. Invented 1876," said Nate, "140. *Specific Philosophical Schools*. Hobbes will be around there somewhere."

I looked up at the shelves, which were all marked with numbers. The nearest one was labelled, '930: History of the Ancient World'.

Answering my unvoiced question, Nate said, "Philosophy is over there. You want the third row from the top." The cowboy pointed towards a dark corner at the back of the shop and paused in thought, "It doesn't usually come up in the games. I don't think I've had anyone ask for that section in years." He glanced around furtively, "You'll need this," he said quietly, handing me a small electric torch and putting his finger to his lips.

I pocketed the illicit tech and thanked him, then wandered over to the rear of the room. I passed close to the man in glasses, who was still the only other customer. He had returned to reading his book. *He looks like he's nursing that coffee*, I thought. I suspected that had been the curse of cafe operation for at least 350 years.

With some difficulty, I shoved one of the heavy ladders over to the corner Nate had indicated. *He should really oil his library more often*, I thought. As I climbed, I peered at a hand-scrawled label in front of me: '100 - Philosophy'. Good, I was on the right track. I ascended another few feet and looked at the next sign: '110 - Metaphysics'. I squinted at some of the subsections: 'Space', 'Time', 'Change'. There might be some useful reading in there for my day job, I thought, but I couldn't see how any of that would help me with this mystery. I continued climbing upwards, hoping the ladder wasn't as antique as it looked. '120 - Epistemology (Theory of Knowledge)', I continued upwards, '130 - Parapsychology and Occultism'. That seemed to be a particularly large section. I glanced at the spines of the books. Most of them were about mesmerism or clairvoyance. I kept clambering upwards.

Finally, a few feet below the ceiling I reached my destination - an area marked, '140 - Specific Philosophical Schools and Viewpoints'. I clung to the wooden rungs and looked down at the floor below me, which suddenly seemed disturbingly far away. I tightened my grip and hoped my epitaph wouldn't read, "Killed in a library" because that would make me sound nerdy. I paused thoughtfully, or like the victim in a whodunit, which wasn't much better - who wanted to be the lifeless corpse in someone else's story?

That made me think of the cloud-haired woman who was shot yesterday. I hoped the pay was decent for such a short role. At least she'd had a last line, "Leviathan! Run!" A little melodramatic but not too bad.

I pondered. If I wanted to get any poignant last words out while I was falling to my death off this ladder, I'd have to yell them pretty quick. I'd also have to make them short. It'd be embarrassing to get cut off half way through. "It's better to burn out, than..." THUD. I mulled the problem. You'd have to prepare a range of potential last lines of various lengths in advance and then select one based on the height you were falling from. I reckoned I was currently at 50 feet, so I'd hit the ground in roughly 2 seconds. Let's face it, my last words would be, "Arghhh!" At least it's a classic.

I turned my attention back to the books in front of me and shifted my weight to take a closer look at the shelf on my right. Suddenly, I heard a cracking noise under my boots. *That's not good*, I thought.

The next moment, my feet were plunging through a snapped rung. I grabbed at the crossbar in front of me in panic as my full weight came down on the step below. One of my boots slipped off the worn surface and I prayed the wood would hold.

Ten seconds later, I was still frozen in place with my heart in my throat.

"Er... Be careful up there?" said Nate from far below.

As health and safety briefings went, it left a lot to be desired.

HOBBES

*Conundra, September
2054*

After gingerly bouncing up and down to check the remaining rungs were solid, I hung over the side of the ladder and heaved it towards H for Hobbes. Nate really needed to take better care of his library equipment.

The light was dim so I dug the contraband torch out of my pocket. At least I hadn't been carrying a lit candle. I precariously hung out into space and ran my finger along the spines: *Hegel, Heraclitus...* Finally, one caught my eye – a thick volume whose title was printed in faded gold lettering: "Leviathan by Thomas Hobbes".

With one hand, I pulled the book out of the tightly packed shelf and stuffed it inside my waistcoat for the journey down the ladder. I carefully made my return descent and, with considerable relief, placed the large tome on a refectory table in front of me. My heart was still racing.

"Looks like you'll be here a while," observed Nate. "Shall I get you another coffee?"

I nodded, then paused, "Actually, make it a decaf."

I sat down and opened the book to its frontispiece – an etching of a huge, crowned figure holding a sword and some kind of staff.

The man who remained the only other customer in the place was still sat at the next table. He cleared his throat and I looked up.

"Nasty, brutish and short," he said.

I glanced at Nate. He wasn't a tall guy, but that seemed uncalled for.

Noting my blank expression, the stranger continued, "It's a quote from Thomas Hobbes: 'And the life of man, solitary, poor, nasty, brutish and short'."

Hobbes sounds a laugh a minute, I thought. I tapped the thick book in front of me, which clearly wasn't going to be a beach read, "Have you studied this?"

He winced, "In depth, actually. It's sort of my job. I'm Alex. Professor Alex Lidenbrock. I'm the curator of the city museum."

I turned my attention to this new information source. He was maybe ten years older than me, although his face was careworn. Museum curation must be a more stressful job than I'd given it credit for.

"Can I buy you another coffee? Perhaps I can ask you some questions about Leviathan?"

◆ ◆ ◆

Five minutes later, I had moved to Lidenbrock's table and beckoned Nate to join us - there were still no other customers for him to worry about.

"What can you tell us about this Hobbes guy?" I asked.

"Thomas Hobbes," the Professor began, "was a seventeenth century philosopher. His area of interest was how societies and governments should be structured and he was famously keen on social contracts. His premise was that for an effective state, individuals must explicitly or tacitly consent to give up some of their freedoms and submit to an authority. In exchange, that authority should protect their remaining rights and maintain law and order. He wrote about it in that book you have in front of you," he gestured at my copy of Leviathan. "It was revolutionary stuff at the time."

"Is your Warlock's Deal a social contract?" I asked. "If you live in Conundra, you have to sacrifice your access to the Panopticon but in exchange the Warlock gives you a story arc?"

"Yes," the cowboy piped up, "and he provides power, food, shelter, clean streets, and all that stuff." I noticed Nate now sounded slightly less Texan and slightly more Birmingham.

"Arguably, Nate, those are from another deal," Alex corrected. "The city of Conundra itself has a contract with WorldGov." He took off his glasses and polished them, "From the start, the Warlock agreed to pay taxes and enforce the planetary laws – including making sure all his subjects were safe, fed and housed. In return, Conundra got protection and financial support from WorldGov, and a voice in making decisions at the global level – if only a small voice. I doubt anyone would feel comfortable living here, or even visiting, if Conundra hadn't submitted to WorldGov's authority. That's the contract that underpins worldwide law and order."

"But you have no deal with the Panopticon." I stated.

"No," said Alex, replacing his spectacles on his nose. "The city council manages stories but for that to work we all have to give up Deus and access to the Panopticon cameras because of the ever present danger of spoilers."

I nodded. It was true. There was no element of surprise with the Panopticon; everything everyone did was wide open – full transparency. That was terrible for controlling the flow of information, which was crucial to suspense.

"Yeah, we understand that," I sighed. "We don't have Deus access for players in our VR worlds either."

"I knew I recognised you!" exclaimed Nate. "Lee Sands! You write the Dystopia games! I used to play those all the time before I moved here."

"The Utopias and Dystopias?" Alex asked. When I nodded he continued, "In that case, you know all about contracts. Don't you commit to certain things for your players?"

I nodded again, thinking about Nemo's public commandments that dictated what he and I were allowed to do in our virtual Worlds. We had needed to sign up to rules or no one would trust our games to have an internally consistent order. It would all descend into chaos and the games wouldn't be worth playing.

Alex paused, "Leviathan was the name Hobbes gave to the ultimate authority which controlled a state. In your game worlds, that's you. In Conundra, the Warlock is the Leviathan."

"That's completely different to the Panopticon nations," I said. "We're a super-democracy. Hobbes wouldn't have liked that - no Leviathan."

"I don't agree," countered Alex, "you still have WorldGov and the State governments and perhaps the Panopticon is a new form of oversight, but it's still authoritarian. With its nudges and social scores the all-seeing-eye enforces behaviour just as much as the Warlock does. The Panopticon may not exert its power through a single sovereign, but Hobbes was fine with that – he never specified you needed one ruler." The Professor paused, "Although, from what I've seen, I'm not convinced Kirby Cross isn't effectively your King." He paused, "Whatever, Hobbes would have been quite happy with the Panopticon, but we should both be grateful. Two orderly societies rose out of the destruction of the Summer. We just achieved them in different ways."

"I'm happy Conundra exists," Nate commented. "At least it gives folk a choice. I don't object to the Panopticon, but I'm glad there's somewhere else to go if I don't want people watching my every move." He grinned, "Maybe I just want some privacy sometimes?"

"That makes no sense," I protested. "You're still being watched! There are cameras all over this place - you just don't personally know the people observing you. You're kidding yourself! You have no privacy here either. At least in the Panopticon nation we accept the truth."

Nate winked, "I find it's easy to ignore people watching you - as long as it's not your Granny."

Alex laughed, "And that's why the Panopticon is such an effective authoritarian regime. It's everyone's Granny, or next door neighbour, or schoolteacher monitoring them all the time. As police forces go, nothing scales quite like it. Everyone behaves themselves."

I considered my recent experiences with people who didn't like the Panopticon. Having Conundra to escape to might give them somewhere to blow off steam - at least the ones without more grandiose plans for change.

On that thought, I grimaced. The London council was still deciding how to use the cleared area around my bombed-out flat. My old building had apparently been "suboptimal". The explosion had drawn the attention of the state to my inefficient land use and now they'd requisitioned the plot. They'd provide me with a new bed somewhere if I needed it. For the moment, I was happy to remain a guest of Kirby Cross in Angelsea.

I wondered if they'd rebuild flats there or not. The ten-year plan for London wasn't finalised yet. With the storms and sea-level rises, we knew we were going to have to relocate the city by 2065. The populace was still deciding between moving somewhere higher or shifting below ground. We reckoned if we could live underground on Mars, we could live undersea on Earth.

Alex continued, "Nate is right, this place serves a purpose. If they don't like it here, our subjects can leave any time they want. Folk who reject the Panopticon don't otherwise have a lot of options. Unless you're some military or scientific superhuman you're not going to qualify to get into space. If you don't like the all-seeing-eye you only have two choices: take your chances in the anarchic states or come to Conundra. You'll be watched here, but not by your neighbours," he grinned, "and the Warlock might be a dictator, but he's a benign one."

I could see Alex's argument, but if there was one thing I was an expert in, it was a dystopia. The trouble with living under a benign dictator was they didn't usually stay nice. What if you stopped being able to trust the authority? What if the sovereign changed – possibly without them even realising?

"Who Watches the Watchers?" I said.

"Quis custodiet ipsos custodes? - Juvenal," said Alex. "Good point."

I left it there. I'd thought it was Captain Picard.

Finally, Nate, Alex and I finished our drinks and stood up. The professor shook my hand and told me to visit him at the museum as soon as I was in the vicinity - there was something he wanted to show me. I promised I would. I suspected I'd get more useful background information from him.

At that moment the door jangled, indicating a new customer was finally entering the place. We turned to see a boy in a bellhop outfit walk in carrying a silver tray.

"Is one of you Lee Sands?" he asked, politely.

I nodded and he hurried over to me and presented the salver. On top of it lay a crisp, white envelope on which was written:

"Urgent: For Your Eyes Only!"

INVITATION

Conundra, September 2054

The envelope was handwritten in a dark, spidery script. Curious, I took the letter and thanked the bellhop. He gave me a swift bow and disappeared quickly out of the shop.

"That's interesting. We've never had that happen before. You must be in a new storyline," Nate said. "Cool."

I opened the envelope and pulled out a thick piece of paper, which was folded in half. *Was this vellum?* I thought. I opened the sheet and stared at a note in the same creepy hand.

My Dearest Lee,

I hope you don't mind my addressing you so informally! I almost feel as if we were friends already!!

When I heard we had a celebrity visiting us, I couldn't wait to show you around our little place myself! The inside tour so to speak!

If you would care to visit the council offices at 1 o'clock this afternoon at One Rubicon Road, I would be delighted to meet you. I literally won't take no for an answer!!!

Yours admiringly,
Concordia Clarke,
Head of Mystery and Intrigue,
The Council of Conundra.

She meant it when she said she literally wouldn't take no for an answer – after the abrupt departure of the delivery boy there was no way for me to decline this invitation.

I showed the letter to the others.

Alex laughed, "Concordia is rather gushing. You'll be 'darlinged' to death. Don't be fooled – I don't think there's anyone who understands the workings of this city better than her." He paused, "She's... extremely competent."

I was sure she was. She must suspect I had ulterior motives behind my holiday. It was astute of her to take a personal look at me and try to ferret out my intent. I, on the other hand, would use the meeting to find out everything I could about her own operations.

This could be fun.

LEVERS

Angelsea, August 2054

What interested me about Conundra was the management. How did the Council operate so many simultaneous, custom storylines? What levers did they pull to control the action?

I reckoned this would be a busman's holiday. I wanted to see how a real place handled the same kinds of scenarios Nemo and I created in our virtual games only with living people, not denizen chatbots, no do-overs, and everything in real time.

Conundra had the randomness of humans to deal with without a reset every twenty four hours. Unlike in a VR game, whatever the guests did there wouldn't be forgotten at midnight. How did that work, I wondered, and what kind of stories did they run? Happy ones? Funny? Sad? Did the tales always play out as intended?

Before the Hot Summer, there had been a TV series or a movie or something about a theme park where the non-player characters were robots. They ended up killing most of the guests for behaving like dicks. We viewers had some sympathy with the 'bots. The premise of the show, however, always struck me as stupid. Why use expensive robotic tech when you could just pay humans to be the NPCs in your park? Guests couldn't kill the staff anymore, but they didn't really kill the robots. Suspension of disbelief was always required by game players.

Actors, a bit of choreography, and some blood packs would have been a much cheaper way to run things - and the failure modes would be a lot more insurable. As a holidaymaker, I'd rather worry about my underpaid human waiter being a bit sulky than my robotic one transforming into a homicidal maniac if I under-tipped them.

In reality though, I knew that was illogical - humans were statistically way more likely to rise up in a bloody revolt than 'bots. The whole premise of that show was silly – rebellion by sentient machines was just a pre-Summer obsession. They should have been more worried about other stuff. AIs running around murdering people was an idiotic plotline.

GOTHIC

*Conundra, September
2054*

Back at the mouth of Dicken's End, I pondered my Leviathan investigations so far. They didn't seem to be getting anywhere, although that had been an interesting conversation. Professor Alex Lidenbrock appeared to be an expert on the history of Conundra, which could be useful – I'd take him up on his invitation to the museum. Before I did that, however, I now needed to visit the offices of the Council of Conundra.

I dug out the city map from my waistcoat pocket and unfolded it. Squinting at the miniscule text, I managed to locate Rubicon Road just to the north of the Roman sector. I didn't need to be there for a few hours, but decided to head in that direction anyway and look around. Lying roughly between my current location and my destination, I saw a tiny area labelled "Gothic". Remembering Phyllida Fogg's comment about the sector, I reckoned I had time to take a quick detour.

◆ ◆ ◆

As I wandered off the main road into the maze of smaller lanes that lead to the Gothic zone, the city became more and more deserted. The streets were increasingly lined with boarded-up shops. Some were covered in purple graffiti that seemed to be mostly pentagrams and other vaguely occult symbols. Pasted onto the walls were faded and peeling posters for mediums and clairvoyants. The whole place made me increasingly uneasy.

I had nearly walked through the small sector when I spotted dim lights in one of the buildings, which appeared to be a bar. I looked up at the sign above the door. Alongside a picture of some huge, unidentifiable sea creature was written the name of the place: "The Leviathan".

Despite it being the late morning of an intensely sunny day, the interior was dark and the place was empty. *The black paint job and filthy windows don't help*, I thought. As I stood gazing around, a thin, scowling woman with dirty hair appeared from the back.

I walked over to sit at the bar and ask her a few questions, then I looked at the stools and decided I could stand.

"Pint of lager?"

She grunted, fetched a grimy glass and started to pour.

"How's business?"

"Busy!" she replied, with what could best be described as a cackle. I must have looked dubious because she continued, "We do a lot of private functions for the Council. More than I can handle if I'm brutally honest," she grinned at me through yellowing teeth.

Brutal I'd believe. Honest? Not so much, I thought, then stopped myself. What was I thinking? I had no right to make a judgment about her based mostly on the quality of her dental work – that was everything the Panopticon rejected. Just because I couldn't see this woman's social ranking didn't mean she was dodgy or hiding anything.

This woman is just part of a different culture, I told myself. Although, given the point of this culture was you could only be judged on your appearance and public actions, I would have invested in hospitality training and a toothbrush.

"I got good news today though," she crowed, "they're sending me a new guy. That'll help." She abruptly switched to complaint, "Not that they ever stay."

I looked at my muddy pint and resolved to hold it but not drink any. Then I thought better of that and decided not to hold it.

"That's interesting. Do they go to another pub to work or do they leave Conundra?" I asked.

"Don't know, don't care," she replied, lighting up a cigarette.

Undeterred, I continued, "This place has an unusual name: The Leviathan," I said, coughing slightly. "Where did that come from?"

"I dunno. I just liked the idea of it y'know? It's like a giant sea monster. I always wanted to have a bar called Godzilla's but the Council wouldn't let me. Not in keeping with the era apparently. They said I could call it 'The Leviathan' instead," she snorted. "Bloody pen pushers. Still, they pay my bills."

"What kind of functions do you offer? Could I hire the place for a birthday party?"

"Yeah. Let me give you our card. Private parties is what we do. I've got a big room at the back. We're really cheap!" she said, proudly. *And realistically*, I thought.

◆ ◆ ◆

Outside again, I wasn't convinced the grubby Leviathan bar had anything to do with my mystery. I wondered what the Council hired it for. Maybe they were just keeping the failing business alive for some reason. This whole area seemed like it was going down the drain. I looked around – maybe it was livelier at night? Was the Council trying to kick start this sector? It was certainly off the tourist trail.

I glanced back up the street I'd just walked down. It was still empty, apart from a tall figure wearing a Homburg hat, leaning against a wall about a hundred yards away. When they saw me looking, whoever it was slipped around a corner and disappeared.

I hesitated for a moment then sprinted after them.

CONCORDIA

Conundra, September 2054

Panting, I reached the corner and looked round. The lane was deserted. Whoever I was chasing had gone. Damn! Had they been watching me go into the bar? Was it part of the Leviathan game?

I leaned against the wall to get my breath back and dug out my pocket watch. Mysterious watchers aside, I'd need to get moving to make my appointment with Concordia Clarke.

◆ ◆ ◆

When I finally found the offices of the Council of Conundra, I was surprised at how cheap and drab-looking they were. I guessed this wasn't a place guests usually visited so there wasn't any point spending money on it. There was no sign outside the building. The address: One Rubicon Road, however, was stuck on the door in plastic letters.

There was an intercom with a single buzzer, so I pressed it and said, "Lee Sands for Concordia Clarke." No response came back, but a long sound indicated the entrance had been unlocked for me. I pushed the door open and stepped inside.

I found myself in a dim corridor. I'd just had time to look up and down it when a cheerful young man appeared from what I presumed was an office.

"Lee Sands?" he asked.

I nodded.

"Great, Concordia is desperate to meet you! Let me show you in."

I followed him up a flight of stairs to a large open plan area filled with desks. People were running around talking enthusiastically and the place was full of whiteboards covered with pieces of paper.

"Welcome to Mystery and Intrigue," he said grinning. "I'm Wade. Wade Scarlet."

"Lee," I said, reaching out to shake his hand. I grinned back.

"I see you've met my deputy," came a penetrating American drawl from the far side of the room.

A tall, thin, and fantastically glossy woman stepped out of a door in the end wall. She swept down on us in a black jumpsuit with implausibly matching hair and a pair of red stiletto heels so narrow I suspected she was punching holes in the carpet. She looked thirty but if you'd told me she was twice that I might have believed you.

Time to turn it on, I thought

I strode over to meet her. "The famous Concordia Clarke, I presume? The Conundran Head of Mystery and Intrigue! You have a remarkable set-up here." I paused confidently - by which I mean slightly longer than most people would risk in case they were interrupted, "I'm extremely impressed."

I gave her my CEO charm-offensive smile: as if we were the only people in the room; I knew my admiration was worth having; and she had all of it. "Are you in charge of everything here?" I asked, providing her with the opportunity to blow her own trumpet under the cover of mild self-deprecation.

If this doesn't work, I thought, *nothing will.*

"Oh no, you're forgetting the Warlock himself! Though he does leave all those dull, day-to-day decisions to me," she laughed, self-deprecatingly, and then paused to make sure it sank in. "Oh, and there are the other department heads of course: romance, pastimes, sanitation. That kind of thing."

I was left in no doubt of their relative importance.

"The Warlock. Certainly," I nodded, giving her a knowing look that suggested we both knew the real score. That was about as much buttering up as I reckoned I could get away with.

She suddenly snapped her fingers, "Wade, have some coffees brought up to us in the Warlock's office. I can tell Lee and I understand one another."

With that, she led me up a second flight of stairs to another enormous room – this one decorated in a faultlessly genteel style. The south wall was glass, giving us a view over the Roman walls and into the bustling centre of Conundra. Looming over the city was the castle and we could clearly see the flag of a golden coin on a field of burnt orange fluttering above it.

She waved me towards a group of leather armchairs, which were arrayed around an embossed mahogany table. Wade arrived with the coffee and Concordia Clarke beckoned him to join us.

While Wade poured out the drinks, I stood and looked through the glazed wall at the milling crowds below: the subjects of Conundra mixing with the vacationing citizens of the Panopticon.

I walked over to the table and sat down. "How closely do you manage them?" I asked, picking up a coffee cup and gesturing towards the people outside, "I'm guessing very closely for the holidaymakers and less so for the subjects?"

"We obviously control the guests fairly tightly," Concordia Clarke agreed, folding herself gracefully into her chair. "They have a schedule for their visit and we need to ensure they stick to it. They usually do," she smiled in satisfaction.

"And your subjects? The manager at my hotel mentioned she helped with the stories for her guests but she was also an occasional player?"

"That's true," Wade piped up enthusiastically. "The subjects are very involved in running games for the visitors, but we do give them their own dramas. Not too often though - that would be exhausting for them," he grinned again, "and for us. Usually, we just maintain good order in their lives. We try to notice when a hint might improve their lot and nudge them onto the right course. We endeavour to make them happier," he paused, "and the city more efficient," he added.

"That's fascinating," I put down my cup, "so you actively try to make their lives better?"

"We're not Gods!" Concordia Clarke laughed. "We can't afford to make our subjects miserable. They pay their taxes and expect an enjoyable life. We have to deliver it or they'll move elsewhere."

The mention of taxes reminded me of something I wanted to check.

"Your marketing materials said you had a very high level of employment. I'm guessing mostly hospitality?" I asked.

"Yes and no," replied Wade. "About half our subjects look after the guests directly. They operate hotels, bars and cafes, cook, clean, all that stuff," he looked at me and I nodded. "Many of the rest of us are council workers like me, who run the games or the city generally. We also have the same kind of people you'd have in any town: doctors, nurses, teachers. We have some agriculture around the city and, of course, we have the actors we use in the dramas," he paused, "and the pseudo-actors."

"Pseudo-actors?"

Concordia Clarke spoke, "Pseudo-actors are people with jobs that exist only to move storylines forward for us. The most obvious example is P.I.s." I looked blank and she snorted in amusement, "Conundra is the only city in the history of the world with more private investigators than hairdressers. Most of them are directly employed by us - we pay them to help flailing guests stick to their schedules and complete their games."

"That's interesting. You use private detectives for that rather than policemen?"

"We try to," said Wade. "The police here are briefed to be earnest-but-bumbling or nice-but-dim. We find guests enjoy it more if they outwit the plodding cops with the aid of a dashing detective. Who wants to have state officials complete their game for them? Where's the fun in that?"

I could see P.I.s were a good solution to struggling players getting stuck half way through a mystery. No one wants to go home before the murderer has been revealed.

"As I'm sure you would guess," said Clarke, "even with Private Eyes to help, our roleplaying scenarios have to be incredibly simple for our guests to follow. We can't make things too complex or they'll never get to the end."

She looked at me and I nodded. In Nemo's and my VR worlds, most of our players were experienced gamers - they did this stuff for hours every day. Even then, we had to be careful not to make it impossibly tricky. I thought about the two guests I'd met in the hotel bar the previous evening. Paul and Esther clearly had no idea what to do in a role-playing game. I suspected the pair would need to be led through their stories by the nose.

"The important thing is often the characterisation rather than the plot," Concordia continued. "You decided to play as yourself, but many people choose a more glamorous persona – no offence," she smiled, charmingly. "They enjoy the chance to be a secret agent or a millionaire-in-hiding or a hidden prince or whatever." She took a sip of her coffee, "The value of our holidays is Conundrans treat our guests as if they really were that character. Our visitors get to escape their mundane lives and experience a fantasy," she paused, "and we help with costumes and styling – if they want that."

"For a fee?"

"Of course. We're all businesspeople here."

I pondered what I'd heard. There was money coming in from the guests, but the overhead of this operation must be huge and most citizens of the Panopticon didn't have a load of cash to spend on holidays. I wondered whether the city was in the red.

"You didn't mention manufacturing among the jobs you had here. I'm guessing you don't export much because you don't have the Panopticon Seal?" I asked.

In the Panopticon states, everything we bought had a seal we could use to view the camera feeds in all the farms, factories, slaughterhouses or transport systems our purchase had passed through. We could verify everything was kosher with our own eyes. After all, by buying their stuff we were agreeing with whatever they did and it became our shared responsibility. With Panopticon cameras everywhere, everyone could police their own supply chain.

"Yes," said Wade glumly, "in theory, we have free trade with the Panopticon states but Panopticoners won't buy our goods without the Seal. We can't afford our own manufacturing industries because we're too small to provide enough demand by ourselves, so we end up importing almost everything. It's expensive."

"We've got some plans to cover that," said Concordia Clarke quickly. "We have started to offer extra, *premium*, services to our guests."

I thought about the flattering letter inviting me here. Was this tour part of some costly head-puffing experience Nemo had bought for me? I thought not. It didn't seem like him and, anyway, any service that involved the time of senior personnel like Concordia Clarke wouldn't scale. I didn't think that was what she had in mind or what Nemo was up to. No, whatever was going on in my brother's brain, I was 100% certain it wasn't about inflating my ego. Knowing him, it was more likely to be the opposite.

I looked at Clarke, who picked up a tablet from the table in front of her and casually glanced at it.

"Oh," she said, "I notice that on your first evening here, you committed a murder."

JOKE

Conundra, September 2054

"You were witnessed chasing one of my actors into an alley, where she was later found shot. No?"

I must have looked momentarily stunned.

"Just my little joke darling," Concordia Clarke laughed. "On your first day, you ran across a trial for one of our new storylines. One of our best actors put on a spectacular death for you! How did you find it?"

"Very convincing," I said, cautiously. Had that been some kind of threat? Or merely her strange sense of humour? For the first time since I arrived in Conundra I cursed how opaque these people were to me. At home, I could have brought up Concordia

Clarke's social scores, viewed her interaction history and built a picture of her character. Here, all I had to go on was what she did in front of me. It was like being blind.

"I'm glad you were impressed," she preened, "it was just an isolated scene. There's nothing else yet, but it was part of a new, more dynamic plotline we're developing. I'm quite proud of how it's working out."

"I thought I might have accidentally elbowed my way into another person's storyline?"

She paused for a moment, "No, it was just a practice run. We might use that plot next year if we can get it right." She looked intently at me, "How was the scene? Was it a good opener, in your opinion?"

I nodded, "Yes, it certainly drew me in."

"Did she give you the note, by the way?" Clarke asked, in an offhand fashion.

"No," I shook my head. "There was no note."

"Oh. Perhaps she went with the final words variant. Was it clear? Did you hear her OK?"

77

Something was wrong. I was used to pumping people for information, but this felt like I was the one being squeezed. I couldn't lie in case the whole thing was legit – maybe I was imagining the uneasy feeling Concordia Clarke was giving me, perhaps I just didn't like the shade of her lipstick. Whatever the reason, my gut said I didn't trust her.

"Actually, it *was* a little garbled. I couldn't really make it out," I said, apologetically. If this was all for real, I hoped my lie wouldn't get the actor in trouble. "Despite that, she was marvelous," I continued, "I'd love to meet her and give her my regards?"

Clarke made a small moue of annoyance, "She's just taken a leave of absence. A sick aunt, I'm afraid. She won't be back until after you've gone."

"What a shame!" I exclaimed.

Concordia Clarke narrowed her eyes. *Damn*, I thought. *I pushed too far and she knows I'm suspicious.* Maybe that was what I'd wanted? To force some action?

"Well darling," she stood up, "I'm going to leave you in the capable hands of Wade, who'll show you around the place. It has been too delightful to meet you in person. We're all huge fans of your dystopian visions. What a tremendous imagination you have! I bet you just wander around seeing plots everywhere."

I got up and Clarke gave me a quadruple air kiss, whilst accidentally stepping on my foot in her stilettos. Fortunately, I was still wearing my steel capped boots or I might have ended up in an accident and emergency department and spent the rest of my holiday in bed. I contemplated again the drawbacks of sandals. Perhaps the fall of the Roman Empire was caused by bread, circuses, and impractical footwear.

She disappeared back down the stairs to what I assumed was her own office. That left me alone with Wade.

"Great," he rubbed his hands together energetically, "let's do the tour!"

TOUR

Conundra, September
2054

Wade Scarlet and I walked back down the stairs to the large room I had seen earlier. He escorted me to the northwest corner, where half the people looked like they were filling out spreadsheets and the other half were talking animatedly to one another.

"Welcome to Fictional Domestic Services," said Wade. "This is our biggest department."

"I'm surprised this comes under Mystery and Intrigue?"

"The butler did it!" laughed Wade. "Actually, we rarely have anyone bumped off by their servants but they are vital to our operations - probably the most important part. We need people who are present all the time and invisible. We occasionally use the microphones and cameras for remote observation but generally it's too expensive to have people watching the feeds. It's cheaper for us to have humans on the ground to observe and act, where they can double up as waiters or whatever. Our domestic staff are all experienced role players. They keep the guests in character and on-track with their storylines as well as look after them. They're the real foundation of Conundra."

Phyllida Fogg, the proprietor of my hotel, sprang to mind. She was in an excellent position to suggest ideas and give clues to guests - a bit like the private investigators were. I briefly wondered why the Council had put expensive observation systems into the city in the first place if they didn't use them. Had they had more subjects to man the system in the past? Or was Wade lying about not using them now?

I couldn't help comparing the Conundran setup to how Nemo's and my own VR worlds worked. We also used innocuous characters like Fogg to help us direct the play and storylines. The difference was, our VR denizens weren't real people like Phyllida. They were just 'bots - they couldn't do anything purposeful themselves. Making decisions on what to change was still an external, human job.

I mused on the current situation with our games. Up until now it had just been me or my brother making interventions and shaping the stories, but we'd decided we needed to hire a team to help us. I suspected the people in front of me would do a very good job of it.

One of the frenetic young people who were rushing past accidentally bumped into me.

"Sorry!" they yelled.

I smiled, "You all look busy."

"Yes we are!" they replied, "Katy hasn't shown up today and everyone's having to cover her stories! It's crazy!"

Wade drew me away, "One of our girls has decided to take off without giving notice. It's annoying, but it happens."

I wondered what Katy looked like.

"How will the others pick up her work? Are all the stories logged?"

"Let me show you our data room!" replied Wade, enthusiastically – it was clear he enjoyed his job.

At the other side of the building, Wade led me into a giant, windowless area full of racks of computers. I winced.

"You look after all your systems yourselves?" I asked. "What if the machines crash or you have a power cut?"

He stared at me blankly while a bespectacled young woman walked up to us.

"Aha!" said Wade in relief. "Meet Montie Scott, our operations expert!"

I shook her hand, "Lee Sands," I said.

"I know," she smiled, "when we saw you come up on the list of visitors this week, we wondered if you'd visit." She looked apologetic, "I'm afraid we don't have quite your budget. Your Worlds all live on the Heavenly Host, I believe?"

I nodded. Omniscience Industries' Heavenly Host data centre had nine nines system reliability.

Neither our games nor our Control VR world should be out of action for more than 1 second in every 20 years – unless some idiot took us down deliberately, of course. Unfortunately, the Heavenly Host was hellishly expensive.

"We don't have all your redundancy but in some ways we're better. We do it old school," she grinned. "We print off the story outlines for the whole week on a Sunday and keep a cardboard folder per guest. Nothing too fatal has ever happened to our systems but, if it did, the DMs are fully capable of running the city for a week off paper. Anyway, the fictional domestic staff all have copies of the weekly plans and can handle most things that come up without head office needing to get involved."

"You call them Dungeon Masters?" I laughed in delight. Dungeon Master or DM was the name of a game manager in Dungeons and Dragons – one of the first fantasy role-playing games. Those early games mostly involved players running around imaginary underground complexes killing orcs. I occasionally enjoyed a session of D&D myself. Nemo was a huge fan and still played every week with Kirby Cross.

Wade smiled broadly, "We tell visitors it stands for Detail Managers."

"How many guests can each DM handle?" I asked.

"During a busy week," said Wade, "it can be up to a hundred but, as we said, most of the day-to-day and hour-to-hour stuff is handled by front line operatives like hotel managers."

I pondered this. That wasn't too bad, I thought, the operation here was fairly slick.

"Concordia Clarke mentioned most guests don't choose to be themselves?"

"Let me show you something," said Wade.

He led me over to one of the computers, sat down in front and navigated his way through a basic-looking user interface.

"There," he clicked and brought up a list on the screen. "We have twelve standard character roles. We just tweak them to fit an individual guest better: gender, age, ethnicity, sector theme - that kind of thing."

I looked at the first few entries on the display:

01 – Plucky hero or heroine.
02 – Wealthy industrialist with a secret mission.
03 – Professor who knows more than he seems.
04 – Mighty warrior with a heart of gold.
05 – Secret agent for a foreign power.

The characters sounded hopelessly clichéd to me.

"Plucky?" I asked.

"Ah, that's what we have you down as," Wade grinned, "some folk, like yourself, don't choose to play a role while they're here. They just act themselves. No avatar – so to speak. We call them PHs. A lot of them are here for a romance."

"And does no one want to be a villain?" I asked, mildly surprised.

"Not really," he replied. "It's a minority requirement. Not a standard storyline. It seems that the vast majority of people would prefer to be a goodie." He looked keenly at me, "We sometimes put on custom packages for slightly less wholesome behaviour," he coughed, "I'd be happy to run some options past you if you're interested? We are, after all, away from prying eyes here."

I had wondered if the city offered specialty services. It made sense. Conundra was still under WorldGov and they couldn't breach the global laws, but WorldGov's strictures were pretty relaxed. Out in the Panopticon, however, we were a conservative bunch and there were plenty of activities it would be embarrassing to pursue - even though they were perfectly legal. I suspected Conundra operated a roaring sex trade for Panopticon citizens.

I shook my head, "Maybe later. You only have a limited repertoire of stories? That would be sensible."

"Yes," said Wade, wandering into the tearoom and refilling his mug from a coffee jug. "We run about twenty off-the-shelf scenarios, which we review every year. We occasionally add a few new ones so our regular guests don't get too bored."

"What kind of plots do you use?"

He looked thoughtful, "We have a classic murder mystery: 'Inspector Calls'. That works very well. We can just switch the motive and location and it seems completely different. We've had guests play the same basic story five times without noticing."

Wade got up from his seat and we started walking again through the offices.

"We have a few simple games like 'Lost Treasure', where players are self-guided." He paused, "We also run a couple of ghost stories. 'Haunted House' is always popular, particularly with a romantic cross-over."

"No science fiction?"

"We haven't got the budget," he replied. "Personally, I can't stand the stuff anyway," then he remembered what I did for a living and looked apologetic. "We do have a few Fantasy storylines. They're quite cheap if we steer clear of dragons."

I nodded, "That's not a bad thing anyway. It's easy to get carried away with special effects."

"We run 'Amulet Quest' in the Celtic zone, 'Sorcerer Quest' in Medieval, and 'Prophecy Quest' for the Saxons," Wade continued.

"Are they very different?"

"Almost indistinguishable," he paused. "Different outfits, of course. That's what's so good about Fantasy – no one ever complains about a lack of originality. It's ideal for us."

I nodded again. Everyone loved a quest.

We clearly both felt I'd learned everything I could from the visit and Wade started walking me back to the entrance.

I pulled down the goggles on my costume and was about to leave when a small, framed photograph on the wall caught my eye. The picture was Concordia Clarke with a man who matched every description I had read of the Warlock: white hair, eyebrows, and signature whiskers. The label below it read: 'Our founder laying the final stone of the rebuilt Roman wall – 2040'.

I pointed at the image, "I didn't realise Concordia Clarke had been involved with Conundra so long?"

"Oh yes," he replied, "the boss has been here since day one."

I opened the door, then suddenly remembered and turned back towards my guide.

"Just one last thing – does the name 'Leviathan' mean anything to you?"

Wade dropped his coffee.

USERS

Angelsea, August 2054

W hat I wanted to know was how he did it. The Warlock had turned a burned out wasteland into one of the most successful holiday destinations in the world, with a premise than was not entirely different from our games.

According to the marketing-speak leaflets, Conundra was a "thriving tourism centre, providing well paid jobs and homes in a vibrant city". People came for an escape from, "Prying, judgmental eyes." By that, I assumed they meant the Panopticon - or rather, the citizens of the Panopticon. I'll admit it; we could be a little prying - and occasionally judgmental.

"The adventure of a lifetime, wrapped up in a week!" With, "No loose ends, guaranteed!" Romances and murders were, apparently, a specialty. The Department of Mystery and Intrigue handled the stories and at the head of the whole organisation was the Warlock. He supervised operations from his "luxurious apartments in the city castle." There was the usual pencil sketch of him with his white hair and moustache.

Something that struck me from the Conundra marketing material was how different their demographic was from ours in our VR games. Their visitors appeared to be all ages and segments and their guests seemed willing to shell out thousands for less than 120 hours of gameplay. Our players were usually male and under 30. They would spend upwards of 500 hours a year in one or other of our VR worlds, but they certainly didn't pay us thousands of Sols. We just made more money because doing everything virtually was way cheaper than doing it for real – I reckoned our margins must be way healthier than theirs.

Our games' current audience was clearly more limited than Conundra's and although our players were more committed, they were less willing to spend their cash. What I wanted to know was what the Warlock's customers were getting from their experience, how we could give that to our users, and how we could get our players to pay more for it. Conundra was just another game – surely there were concepts they were using successfully that we could borrow.

Apart from the obvious real vs virtual thing, the main way Conundra differed from our games was in the level of personalisation. Their stories seemed more tailored to an individual. Nemo and I essentially provided a single mystery for everyone to solve in each of our VR worlds. Conundra appeared to be advertising a new plot for every one of ten thousand weekly visitors.

Was it the uniqueness that their guests loved or the physical presence? Was it the total immersion? The enforced attention? Was it something else entirely? I planned to look at what they were up to and "be inspired" by some of their ideas. In other words, what's a holiday without a little industrial espionage?

SPF

Conundra, September 2054

"Damn!" said Wade. "What a klutz I am." He bent down and started mopping up his spilled drink with a handkerchief, "What was that name again? I didn't quite catch it."

"Leviathan," I repeated.

"No, no. It doesn't ring any bells with me."

◆ ◆ ◆

I left Wade sponging the carpet and walked back onto the sunny streets.

I took a path that followed the outside of the restored Roman wall around the centre of the city. I'd read they rebuilt using the original material - a kind of compacted clay called septaria stone. Like everything else in Conundra, I thought, it was an astonishingly convincing fake. Without the Panopticon, how could anyone know what was true and what was a lie here? You could hide anything in this place.

With that in mind, I considered my encounter with Concordia Clarke and Wade Scarlet. I reckoned it could hardly have been more sinister. Why had they really wanted to see me? My gut told me Clarke was lying about my encounter with the murdered woman. Why? Had something gone wrong with the performance and the woman really had been killed? I'd thought that warning bullet for me was dangerously close. Were they trying to cover up an accidental death?

It was possible, I thought. An incident like that might destroy Conundra. On the other hand, was I just imagining the whole thing in a frenzy of distrust, triggered by not having the all-seeing-eye to ask? Or was this all set up by Nemo to give me a tough mystery to get my teeth into? That would actually be just like him.

I considered the photograph I'd just seen of Concordia Clarke and, presumably, the Warlock. It opened up a lot of questions. She was clearly part of the group that created the city. How much did she care about the place? Enough to stage a cover up? Had she known the Warlock from before the destruction of Colchester?

I wondered how she'd been recruited. Maybe she herself had been the recruiter! What were the real names of the Warlock and Clarke before the founding of the city and what had they done before the Hot Summer? I decided if I wanted to find out more about them I needed to take up Professor Alex Lidenbrock's invitation to visit the museum.

After a mile of furious walking and thinking, I found myself in front of a huge entrance into the central sector. I stared through the open gateway at the Roman zone.

Apparently, Conundra had based their re-creation on Pompeii. Floods of toga-wearing tourists were streaming in and out of low, stone buildings. Almost all of them were eating ice creams, holding maps, and pointing at things - I suspected they were mostly on some variant of the "Treasure Hunt" storyline.

Distracted for a moment, I pondered whether the Romans had really had ice creams. I muttered grumpily about not having Deus to ask, then remembered to look at my guidebook. It told me that the Emperor Nero had eaten them. Sucking an ice lolly while Rome burned, I thought, would have been more ironic than playing the violin - he'd missed a supervillain trick there.

I felt a sudden tap on my shoulder and spun round.

"Dave the Celt!" I exclaimed.

"So your quest brought you down here after all?"

"Indeed it did. Fancy an ice cream? It seems to be what the Romans did."

"Well," he grinned, "when in Rome."

◆ ◆ ◆

Ten minutes later, we were sitting on a stone bench watching a knight in full armour stride past us towards the castle.

"Bloody hell, he must be hot," I said.

"At least medieval knights didn't have to wear sun cream," Dave commented, squirting some onto his knees.

It was a good point. I suspected plate mail had a decent SPF.

"Did you get your shopping done?" I asked.

He pulled a stick of rock with Conundra written through it out of his satchel, and then a fridge magnet of a man being hung, drawn and quartered with, 'Welcome to the Middle Ages' written underneath.

"For my niece."

"So, tell me about your storyline so far," I said.

◆ ◆ ◆

Dave told me everyone in the Celtic camp was involved in a rebellion against their Roman overlords, but to win they had to find some bit of jewellery that could only be worn by the rightful ruler.

"It's plausible," I said.

"Yeah," Dave replied, "my sister has a pair of earrings like that. If you don't have the right cheekbones, you can't pull them off."

"Can your sister?" I asked, curiously.

"Not really," he replied, "I don't say anything."

Dave felt he had more of a run-around-hitting-things role in his game than a speaking one. He didn't get the impression he would end up finding the Amulet of Destiny and claiming the royal crown. Not that he minded - the beer was good.

I wondered how far a player could change their own storyline in Conundra. Presumably, I thought, the person who would be King or Queen had paid a premium for that and would be difficult to shift. I suspected Dave was on a basic holiday package. Still, there might be a way to upgrade his character by effectively creating a new role for him on top of his existing one. Could he sneak in his own story on top of the official one, I wondered, by selling it to the other guests directly? I suspected he could - if it was in keeping with the rest of the game.

"You should issue a challenge," I said.

Dave looked blank.

"In real life, what competition do you reckon you'd win, given the rest of the guests in the Celtic camp?" I looked at his bulgingly impressive biceps, "Strength? Axe throwing? You could issue a challenge to the Royal Champion or, if there isn't already one, propose a tournament tomorrow to choose one."

He looked intrigued.

I continued, "I bet if you make it an interesting storyline and ask for a role that isn't already defined, but is easy to add, you'll get your competition. Especially if most of the guests are sitting around drinking beer, getting into trouble, waiting for the big fight scene at the end?"

"That *is* pretty much what we're doing," said Dave. "A lot of the other guys are big though," he mused, "it wouldn't be a walk over."

He stood up, raised his huge axe above his head and shook it. He was six foot eight and built like a giant, shiny action figure.

"Do I look like a Royal Champion?"

"Knock 'em dead." I replied.

HOLIDAY

Angelsea, August 2054

I n the ward of Beaumaris Castle, a pleasant breeze was blowing. As usual in North Wales, it was a hot, sunny day. Thankfully, someone had retracted the storm dome that normally covered the building. I looked around at the beautiful HQ of Omniscience Industries and the home of their CEO, Kirby Cross. For the past six months, it had also been home to Nemo and me.

I sat at a shady table under one of the courtyard's many trees with my friend and the newest Panopticon Senator, Laura Close. She poured us tea from a pot that had clearly been rescued from the castle's pre-Summer gift shop.

"Congratulations on your election," I told her.

"It seemed sensible to have a formal Panopticon presence on Angelsea. I've bought a small place in the village and I'll mostly stay there. It's easier on my old bones than jangling around in a horse and cart."

I'd ridden a few times in the cart that Laura and her companions used to use to tour the country. I preferred my bike, which actually had some suspension.

"Your brother tells me you are taking a holiday?" she said, "I'm glad to hear it."

"So am I," I replied. "This will be the first test of our partnership with Omniscience. Conundra is only a few hundred miles away," I grinned at Laura, "if it all goes horribly wrong, your Panopticon can send emergency transport for me."

After Nemo and my misadventures the previous spring, our real time world simulator, Control, had been named as critical infrastructure by the Panopticon. To comply with our new status, we had been required to create fully resilient systems around the sim. That included having backup personnel who could cover for Nemo or me if we were ill or incapacitated or just decided to go on vacation.

Rather than build that new support system from scratch, we'd agreed to piggyback off Omniscience Industries systems and processes. Their famous Deus chatbot had been critical infrastructure for more than a decade – they knew how to comply with the rules. Fortunately, the Panopticon had agreed to cover all our expenses as long as Control remained free for its citizens.

"It will be good to see how robust things are in your absence," Laura commented.

I nodded, glumly. On the bright side, the cultural nationalisation had allowed me to take a holiday, which was probably good. On the downside, no longer being able to charge for any part of our flagship product had put a significant dent in my bank balance.

The positive result of becoming more trusted and closer to the Panopticon, however, was they'd given Nemo and me access to improved data. Control was now more all-seeing than ever. I was torn – our product was better but we couldn't directly make any money out of it. I needed to think of something.

"I'm frustrated to leave the weather control stuff I've been working on," I sighed, "I do need some distance on it though."

WorldGov was bankrolling Samara, a project to extract energy from air masses – specifically building storms – and I was helping with the predictive modelling. Progress was mixed. I was worried we were still years off and although the real-world storms weren't getting worse, they weren't improving either. They were still wiping out too much of our global recovery every year and the constant stream of new refugees was a strain on all the states. At least it was easier to handle the new folk now we were all, first-and-foremost, Panopticon citizens but it was still hard work.

We remained on a war footing, with our adversary being the air around us. All the new tree planting we were doing was useful but mostly it was a PR exercise – the trees wouldn't have much impact for decades and if they caught fire we were back to square one. The grass and algae projects were better – the topsoil and seabed storage was faster, more permanent and less flammable. Nevertheless, we were going to be battling the weather for a long time and the annual worldwide death toll was still way too high.

Changing the subject, Laura ventured, "While you are in Conundra, maybe you can do some poking around for us?"

"For the Panopticon?" I asked, surprised.

"Yes," she continued, "we really don't know as much about that city as we'd like. Any impressions you form would be interesting to us. In particular, we're keen to understand what drives people to leave the Panopticon states and migrate to Conundra. Is it just nostalgia or something more systemic – something that might indicate a flaw in our supernation? Anyone who chooses to leave the Panopticon is a failure on our part. We'd like to know why it happens." She paused, "We're also very interested in this Warlock person. You know, we can't find a single photograph of him."

Spying for the Panopticon as well as industrial espionage? It sounded like my vacation would be interesting.

MUSEUM

Conundra, September
2054

The mighty Dave strode off in the direction of the Celtic camp, leaving me to continue my own quest. If I wanted to find out more about the founding of Conundra, the obvious next step would be to go and speak to Professor Alex Lidenbrock and I had been planning to do that anyway. I knew the museum was in the castle, which I could see looming above the single storey buildings of the Roman zone. I started walking in that direction.

Before the Hot Summer, the city's Norman castle had sat in the middle of a large park. The position had let it escape the fire relatively unscathed. In the new city of Conundra, guest space was at a premium so the park was gone. Clay and stone buildings now pressed right up against the keep. The renamed Castle Conundrum was only 800 years old rather than two thousand, but it was genuinely historical. I guessed that was good.

At the front of the tower, there was still a small moat and the entrance lay across a drawbridge that was crowded with guests from every era. I stood in thought. Even though I was looking at the people through the glass of my goggles, there were no AR popups floating above them like there would be at home. I didn't know if they were rich or poor, good or bad. If they paid their taxes on time or were considerate cyclists. I didn't know whether they were welcome house guests, decent plumbers, good for a random chat in the pub, or if I could lend them a tenner and ever get it back. Basically, I didn't know anything about them. I couldn't even judge them by their dress sense because they were all in costume. I wondered how people could live like this.

Shaking my head in incomprehension, I walked across the drawbridge and into the castle.

◆ ◆ ◆

Inside the building, there were crowds of visitors and a lot of purple drapes. Teams of actors were probably hidden behind them waiting to jump out at the right moment. I wondered if the Warlock really lived here. It seemed rather busy to be anyone's actual home.

I walked up to a helpful centurion, who pointed me at the small door to the museum. It was half hidden by one of the curtains. I pulled them aside, turned the handle and went through.

On the other side, I was assaulted by a vision of glass-fronted cabinets in every direction. The small room was packed, floor to ceiling, with towers of glazed curiosities: golden torcs, urns, a few swords that Dave might have considered more puny than Punic. Actually, I suspected Dave was not the punning type - he was more the hitting-punners-with-an-axe type. And who could blame him.

I peered at a pair of earrings in one of the displays and wondered if they too would have defied Dave's sister and her cheekbones. I'd previously had no idea such a problem existed. With the earrings was a collection of old-looking gold and silver armlets, rings, and coins. The cabinet was labelled 'The Fenwick Hoard – Camulodunum'.

"I see you've found our most famous collection," came a voice from behind me.

I turned to see Alex Lidenbrock walking towards me from a small office.

"Camulodunum?" I asked.

"It was the Ancient Roman name for Conundra," Alex replied. "The town was built around AD 40 as a Roman legionary base – right after the conquest of Britain. Camulodunum is a Latinization of the Celtic name for the location, which meant the stronghold of Camulus - the Celtic God of War. Despite the nod, Camulus took his revenge for the invasion: the original city was destroyed by Celts."

I'd clearly caught Alex in an expository mood, which was exactly what I wanted.

"'The Fenwick Hoard?' Sounds swashbuckling," I said.

"It is and it isn't," Alex replied, removing his spectacles and polishing them on his handkerchief. "The name actually refers to a department store.

The hoard was discovered during a shop renovation in 2014. That was before I was born, but my parents lived in the city back then." He looked wistful, "The idea of buried treasure always fascinated me. It was why I became an archaeologist in the first place - and a bit of a detectorist." He smiled at my confusion, "Someone who wasted too much of their childhood combing the countryside with a metal detector, hoping to find some hidden trove. No, the interesting thing about the Fenwick Hoard isn't its name - it's how it got there."

BOUDICCA

Conundra, September 2054

For nearly twenty years, Prasutagus the Iceni chief of an area north of the new city of Camulodunum led a happy and prosperous coexistence with his Roman overlords. In AD 60 he sadly died, leaving his realm to his grieving daughters whose names are lost in antiquity. The daughters would be watched over in their rule by their loving mother.

The Roman Emperor Nero, however, had other plans. He put down his famous evil ice lolly and devised a plot. The Empire decided to take the death of Prasutagus as a pretext to renege on their peace treaties with the Iceni Celts, seize their lands, rape the dead King's daughters and flog his bereaved Queen.

The wronged mother was tall with tawny hair hanging down to her waist. She had a harsh voice and a piercing glare, and her name is not lost to history: it was Boudicca.

Queen Boudicca of the Iceni led a coalition of furious Celtic tribes in revolt against their Roman occupiers. Their first target was the unfortified town of Camulodunum. The Roman governor, Gaius Suetonius Paulinus, was away with his armies fighting on what is now the island of Angelsea. At the time, it was a western holdout of British rebels. He was in no position to defend the city.

Knowing of the approaching Celtic armies, the city's lack of defenses, and her likely fate, a Roman citizen of Camulodunum gathered her gold and silver and buried it under the floor of her house. Nearly two millennia later, it was discovered by chance when a department store decided to redecorate and called the Fenwick Hoard.

"What happened to the Roman woman?" I asked Alex.

"There were only two hundred troops in the city. They were easily overwhelmed and the place was methodically destroyed by Boudicca and her army. They besieged the last defenders in the Temple of Claudius for two days and then sacked it. She killed every inhabitant: man, woman, and child, and finally burned the city to the ground." He paused, "There is still a thick layer of ash under Conundra, left over from Boudicca's rebellion two thousand years ago. The Fenwick treasure was found in a clay pot underneath that ash."

I pondered the lessons of the tale. "It was a mistake to piss her off," I said.

MAXIMS

Conundra, September 2054

"You call this place Conundra," I stated. "Conundra, Camulodunum. Is the similarity a coincidence?"

"The Warlock named the city and is, I believe, interested in Roman history." Alex shrugged, "Perhaps there's a connection."

We were sitting in his office while he poured mugs of tea. I looked around at the snug room, which was neatly lined with books and paper files. Professor Lidenbrock was clearly an orderly guy. On one of the shelves I noticed a worn copy of, 'Journey to the Centre of the Earth'.

"You're a Jules Verne fan, of course!" I exclaimed, "Professor Lidenbrock – from the book. So, what was your real name before you came to Conundra?"

"I've been here so long, I can't even remember," he picked up his cup. "Just call me Alex."

I realised this was my opening to ask about Concordia Clarke.

"How early did you arrive? Did you see much of the founding of the city?" I asked. "At the Rubicon Road office, I saw a photograph of Concordia Clarke laying the final stone of the Roman wall with someone I assume was the Warlock. Do you know them both?"

"You do ask a lot of questions," he looked amused, "but I'll try to answer them for you: it was very early, yes I did see the founding, and Concordia and the Warlock have been colleagues of mine for a very long time. Does that tell you what you need?"

Given that, I had to assume Alex was a friend of Concordia Clarke's – it sounded like they'd worked together for at least fifteen years. Nevertheless, my gut told me to confide in him. I would have to trust someone in this place or I wasn't going to get anywhere. Alex had the double benefit of clearly possessing useful information and seeming relatively normal. Most vitally, his tea wasn't bad and I quite liked his office.

"I had a very odd interview with Concordia Clarke this afternoon and got the feeling she was lying to me about something I saw when I first arrived."

I told Alex about the woman at the station, the shooting, and her choked last words. I also repeated what Clarke had said about my accidentally stumbling on a practice scene.

He sat in silence for a few minutes, "Hence your question at Nate's about Leviathan?"

I nodded. He remained still for another moment.

Suddenly, he looked directly at me and said, "Concordia can be a strange woman," he paused as if considering his words. "Before the Hot Summer, she was a very successful film director. Of course, it was clear that Hollywood was never going to be the same after '36 – it felt like all we saw were propaganda movies for years."

I didn't get the chance to watch much TV or film back then.

"You might have been too young to pick up on it. After the Hot Summer, we were all on a precipice. Humanity had suffered near-apocalypse and it was clear everything was going to have to change. It just wasn't yet obvious how. Money was ceasing to have value because the nations were wobbling and all the usable currencies were state-backed."

I nodded understanding, although Nemo and I had been in the refugee camps back then so we'd had no money to spend anyway.

Alex continued, "We all lived on goodwill, bartering and handouts for a while. Everyone was trying to guess who would be good for their debts." Alex removed his glasses and polished them again, "We were desperate for a new way to run things that we could all get behind fast. Kirby Cross's team at Omniscience came up with a form of collectivism based on the Panopticon.

People listened to him because Omniscience Industries was one of the only stable organisations left. Kirby's plan involved a massive wealth and land transfer to WorldGov," Alex peered at me, "and Omniscience Industries was willing to pay the new taxes because Kirby was the CEO and majority shareholder. That made it harder for other corporations to object. Plus, the taxes bankrolled something we all wanted - a stable state and a currency again in WorldGov's Sol. Kirby's idea was radical and it was a huge risk."

He grimaced and dragged his hand through his hair, "The Warlock didn't want the Omniscience plan to be the only one, because it might not work. It might still fail," he replaced his spectacles, "so he created an alternative."

That was quite a monologue, I thought. *Alex clearly cares a hell of a lot about this - or he likes the sound of his own voice. And who doesn't?*

"I didn't think it was entirely Kirby. Wasn't the new world order everyone's decision?"

Alex raised an eyebrow, "Whatever you want to believe. Anyway, post-'36 all those wartime-spirit movies Hollywood made to calm people down didn't play to Concordia's strengths. Her particular talents were going to waste until Conundra came along - the city saved her." He paused, "What I'm saying is Concordia is easy to misconstrue but she cares more than anyone about this city. I don't believe she would ever do anything to endanger it."

The trouble was, even if that were true it didn't tell me anything. If the council had accidentally shot someone and were covering it up, Concordia Clarke might be lying to save the city. According to Alex's description, that would be entirely in character.

He must have caught my expression, "I realise that doesn't rule anything out," he said, apologetically. "I can do some quiet asking around for you?"

"Thanks that would be great. Perhaps I can drop back again tomorrow to see what you dig up?" I sighed, "You know, this would be a whole lot easier if I could see Concordia Clarke's social scores like I could back in the Panopticon."

"No spoilers." said Alex.

"I understand why social scoring is outlawed in Conundra, it's just bloody hard not knowing if I can trust someone!"

"The problem with asking whether you can trust a person is: trust them to do what?" Alex responded. "A single score is meaningless. Take me, you could definitely trust me to look after your cat, but absolutely not to borrow your car - I was a terrible driver even before the Summer and no one's going to be crying that I was taken off the roads." He paused, "The Council does maintain some internal trust ratings. They're just not public. We use them to decide which parts to assign to people - some of our subjects can handle a difficult role like a complex villain and others are best off sticking to playing themselves. We need to know which is which when we cast a game." He smiled ruefully, "If it helps, I happen to know Concordia is an excellent actor."

That didn't really help.

I thought about Alex's words. He was out-of-date. We were now far more sophisticated in our use of scoring. We had a whole range of rankings because single scores were indeed meaningless.

Omniscience Industries was already working on how Deus could display the different types of rank. The idea was to personalise. I might really care how good a gardener you were. Someone else would be more interested in your credit history. Your AR popups needed to be tailored to your observer.

"In the Panopticon, we believe transparency is the basis of society. If I know all about you - the truth - I can draw my own conclusions about whether to trust you. I can look at any of your social scores but I still don't rely on them - they're just a convenience. What I rely on is all the raw data we have on you so I can see for myself. It's my duty to make my own decisions. Here in Conundra, I don't know anything about Concordia Clarke so I can't make an informed judgment - I just have to guess what she's like from surface appearances. That's massively flawed."

I thought about Clarke and her stiletto-thin heels. I was innately suspicious of anyone who could kill me with their own footwear but that was illogical. An angry-enough Dutch person could bludgeon me to death with a clog; I was sure there were trained people in the world who could murder me with a flip-flop. I suspected the ability to weaponize an item of clothing was more about the individual and their current state of mind than their observable shoe style, which actually told me nothing.

Alex broke me out of my introspection, "The Panopticon state is obsessed with judging everything! And you're fooling yourself, I bet most of you entirely go on the scores you're handed and don't look any further."

"Judgment is what makes us human. It's our whole purpose! Exerting our judgment is what we do in the Panopticon states!"

Although I was defending us, Alex did have a point. I'd recently realised not every citizen viewed the data they were handed critically. That was something Nemo and I did by default because we were used to seeing how often mistakes crept in. If we saw something we didn't believe we always checked with another source. I was, however, worried there was a lack of that skepticism among the general citizenry and I wasn't sure what we should do about it.

I'd talked the problem over a few times with Laura and Kirby Cross. We could certainly try to improve the systems so fewer bugs crept in, but there would always be errors. I'd rather people trusted their own judgement - if they saw something dodgy, I wanted them to know how to investigate for themselves. That was something we needed to cover more in our ongoing-education curriculum.

"You're all so... so Kant!" Alex shook his head.

"Hang on," I said, "back in the coffee shop, Nate mentioned Kant as well. I don't see the relevance?"

I knew Immanuel Kant was an old philosopher but he wasn't the one who'd invented the Panopticon - that was Jeremy Bentham. Bentham came up with the idea as a way to run a perfect prison. Of course, the Panopticon supernation was not a jail.

My question obviously switched Alex back to Professor-mode, "Kant was a German Enlightenment philosopher who was as fanatical about the truth as you lot. He even argued you shouldn't tell a lie to a murderer to save someone's life because that would be depriving the killer of their human agency!"

I thought about that. I could see where Kant was coming from. Lying wasn't worse than murder but as a single event I might argue it was as bad. I guessed Kant was saying that being alive without a true view of the world and the ability to make clear judgements from it was as bad as not existing at all. From that perspective, lying to someone was destroying the vital part of what made them human as much as murder. Though, I had to admit, it was less final. If I asked someone whether my new haircut looked good, I'd rather get a phony complement than be mowed down with a submachine gun. Kant clearly didn't feel the same. I suspected he'd learned not to ask people their opinions on his outfits.

"That's interesting," I said, "I quite like the sound of Kant though I suspect he wouldn't have been the ideal dinner guest."

"'Morality is not how we may make ourselves happy, but how we may make ourselves worthy of happiness - Immanuel Kant' No, I wouldn't expect any nice comments about your dessert," Alex responded. "But, he was interesting. In some ways, the Panopticon was invented by him. He wasn't only keen on full disclosure. He also wanted us to treat people as ends rather than means, and he was very against unscalable behaviour - don't do it if everyone can't."

"Unscalable stuff is what we all turned against after the Summer. Most of the demerits we get in the Panopticon are for things like that – speeding or not keeping your skills up."

"I always wondered about that," asked Alex, "can you just pay a fine and dodge those demerits?"

"No," I replied, "we learned that lesson: 'punishable by a fine means allowed for rich people'."

"Like you?"

"Indeed, like me. Sometimes there's a fine as well as demerits but in that case the fine is always based on wealth so the level of pain is the same for everyone. We do still do unscalable stuff though. Like the Moon base and the Mars project. Not everyone can go there."

"Those are WorldGov projects, not Panopticon ones. Only WorldGov has that kind of budget. As I understand it though," he said, resuming his professorial demeanour, "those projects are highly controlled. We all agreed that only a small number of our representatives would take humanity into space - it will never be for most of us Earthlings."

"You can't buy your way into space either," I commented, "it's strictly by-invitation: specialists only. Even then, it's highly rationed. There's an iron-clad rule - no matter who you are, you only get one trip out of a gravity well per person. If I were to leave Earth and go to Mars, that would be a one-way trip. I could never leave Mars again for any reason. I couldn't pay my way back. It's the Martian Deal."

"And sensible, given the mega joule cost of getting a human into orbit from any planet," Alex agreed.

I nodded, "You have to mean it because it's your only shot. Irrevocable."

I was glad we were keeping going with Mars and the Moon. There had been a tough debate over investing in the space programs while there was still so much work to do on Earth. We all decided humanity needed a vision beyond just fixing what we'd broken and staying alive. We also still needed a backup plan for some of humanity to survive if we lost this war.

"I reckon Kant was a good guy. Sounds like we should all listen to him."

"Be careful," Alex retorted, "just because he wrote about morality doesn't necessarily mean he was good himself. Have you heard of the Roman philosopher Seneca?"

"Didn't he write essays about how to live a good life?"

"Oh yes," Alex said, "Seneca wrote a great deal about morality. He was also Nero's advisor during Boudicca's rebellion. Worse, he was one of the primary causes. He and his cronies forced loans on the Celts in the wake of the invasion – when Britain was still a Roman gentrification project. Then, when Nero lost interest in that scheme, Seneca and the other moneylenders foreclosed, rendering the Celts destitute. No one knows how much money Britain owed, but Seneca was in for at least 40 million sesterces, which would have paid for about 45,000 legionaries back then. The Iceni rebellion was as much about Seneca and his sudden loan recall as Boudicca and her personal wrongs. The revolt probably killed at least 200,000 Romans and Britons."

"Blimey," I said. "Did Seneca get any comeuppance?"

"He wrote a hugely successful book on morality – about how wealth could be an instrument of virtue."

"What a total wanker. Kant should have punched him out."

"They were seventeen hundred years apart," Alex responded. "I'm not sure Kant had the reach."

"So Seneca never paid any price for his part in the rebellion?"

"Actually, a few years later his colleagues got sufficiently sick of him they forced him to commit suicide."

"Wow," I said, "a literally toxic work environment."

I thought about the Council offices I'd just visited. Were they a toxic environment - figuratively or otherwise?

Suddenly, I remembered a question I'd wanted to ask, "By the way, what kind of films did Concordia Clarke direct in Hollywood before the Summer?"

"Oh, didn't I say?" said Alex. "She made horror movies."

FAREWELL

Angelsea, September 2054

"Are you sure you don't want me to give you a lift?" asked my little brother, solicitously.

That's uncharacteristically helpful, I thought. *What's Nemo up to now?*

"Of course not!" I replied, "You know using personal transport kills your social scores!"

I was planning to take the bus to Manchester, the train to London and then another one to Conundra. It would take me a day but I could work while travelling.

He shrugged, "Who cares about demerits? We're not at school."

"You may be happy with the interpersonal ratings of a serial killer with a bad haircut," I replied, "but I like to talk to people who aren't poised to flee."

"The thing about a shame culture is it can only control you if you feel any," my brother smirked. "I like my scores. Fewer distractions. It's revolting the way strangers come up to you in the street for a chat," he shuddered.

Nemo was clearly exaggerating. Having players talk to me was one of our most successful community marketing strategies. If I had a terrible social score it would cost us a fortune.

"So, are you looking forward to your holiday?"

That question was also way too pleasant, I thought. *He definitely wants something.*

"Why? Do you have a mission for me too?" I asked, suspiciously.

He paused, "No, no. Just pay attention will you? Like you normally do."

Nemo obviously had some scheme in mind, but he clearly wasn't going to tell me what it was yet. I considered ferreting it out for myself in the Control sim but I couldn't be bothered. I reckoned he'd update me eventually.

He looked slightly guilty, "And, err, be careful."

VISITOR

Conundra, September 2054

That evening, I arrived back at Fogg's hotel and wandered into the bar. Esther and Paul were sitting at a table animatedly discussing something. I didn't like to disturb their holiday romance. They had, after all, booked it. They caught sight of me and waved.

"How was your day?" said Paul.

"Interesting," I replied. "How about you?"

"It was so exciting!" cried Esther. "We were on our way to the park this morning..."

"Did Phyllida suggest that?" I asked, curious about the mechanism of story execution.

Esther paused, "Oh yes, she did - now you mention it. Anyway, we were on our way to the park when we passed a very old woman in a long cloak, who had fallen in the street. We helped her up and she thanked us profusely and left - but we realised she'd dropped her locket!"

"I ran around the corner to catch her but she'd completely disappeared," added Paul. "It was very mysterious."

Esther continued, "Anyway, we opened the locket and inside it we found an old photograph and an ancient map!" she smiled glowingly at Paul. "Phyllida had the idea we could follow the map in the hope we might find the old lady and return her things. We've been puzzling out clues all day. It's great fun."

That sounded well-constructed. They should be fairly self-guided for the rest of the week, I thought, and Phyllida can help again if they get stuck. It was a good set-up. I was impressed.

"That's amazing!" I responded cheerfully. "I was at the museum. You should visit. I've also heard there's going to be a big competition at the

Celtic camp tomorrow to find a Royal Champion. I'm sure Phyllida will know all about it."

"Excellent!" said Paul. "We'll ask her."

I left them gazing into one another's eyes and walked over to the bar. I reckoned if I talked up Dave the Celt's Royal Challenge, it was more likely the Council would come up with a prize and he'd get his magical Belt of Champions – or some such dodgy accessory. I wanted to see if I could bend a storyline and I reckoned it wouldn't hurt to have a higher status friend in the Celtic camp. You never knew when these things would come in handy.

"Hi Phyllida, how are you?" I asked, and decided to cut to the chase, "I'm really looking forward to the Celtic Royal Challenge tomorrow."

She looked confused.

"I heard about it in the Roman Zone. Apparently, there's some Belt of Champions to be won. It sounds great. Paul and Esther are going."

Phyllida smiled, "Well, I hadn't heard about that, but I agree it's a good idea. The Celts do tend to lounge about drinking all week. It'll do them good to have something to occupy them. I'll look into it and let my other guests know." She paused, "Gosh, I nearly forgot. You have a visitor."

"A visitor?"

"He's in the private lounge," she pointed, "with a decanter of my good whisky. He's made a considerable..." she paused, "effort with his costume."

I wondered who on Earth it could be and ordered a cold beer. While I waited for Phyllida to draw my pint, I fanned myself with a beermat - it was a sweltering evening.

◆ ◆ ◆

Holding my drink in one hand, I pushed open the door to the private bar. The place had a deep green tartan carpet and dark oak panels and I could just see a hatted head over the back of a wingback chair by the window. As I got closer, I made out a figure in a deerstalker, wearing a heavy tweed Inverness cape, and holding a pipe.

"What are you doing here!" I exclaimed. "You must be boiled alive in that get up."

"Verisimilitude is everything," Nemo replied, "and I'm on a case... By the way, 'Hello Lee, I'm you'."

I stopped and sat down in the chair next to my brother. That was our joke: a coded request for a full debrief on the current situation. *This is odd*, I thought, *since when has Nemo ever wanted to chat about holidays?*

"But, before we start," he said, "let's guarantee ourselves a little privacy. I've already spotted the microphones in the potted plants." He fished around in his voluminous pocket, dug out a small broadcasting device and turned it on. "That should scramble everything within earshot. It'll be noticeable on the recordings but what are they going to do, shoot us?" he chuckled.

It wasn't out of character for Nemo to act strangely, so I humoured him by providing a complete rundown of everything that had happened to me since I stepped off the train the previous evening. I also told him that, at least according to Wade Scarlet, the city's survcillance systems weren't monitored.

"So, what's going on?" I demanded when I'd finished my update, "You obviously had some motive for getting me to come here – beyond giving me the chance to eat ice cream."

"You genuinely did look terrible. I really reckoned you needed a holiday. However, as you've probably guessed, you're going to have to cut your break short. So," he smirked, "your looks are unlikely to improve."

I sighed. Nemo was reliably annoying.

"I did indeed have an ulterior motive for buying your ticket here," he continued, "I wanted you to get a feel for the place with no preconceptions and give me an objective situation report."

Nemo clearly wanted to drag me into one of his deranged capers. What was it this time? I was sick of using my weekends to investigate rumours of alien landings or abominable snowmen. Suffice it to say, we had seldom found any truth out there. Another E.T hunt had not been my plan for this week. I sat back in my chair and folded my arms.

"What kind of preconceptions might I have had?" I asked, pointedly.

My Sherlock-a-like companion took a puff on his pipe, which was apparently full of washing up liquid because a large bubble rose from it and floated off above our heads.

"I suspect your new friends in Conundra are bumping off their guests."

LOSERS

Angelsea, June 2054

Back in June, while I had been busy with weather control in Utopia Six, my brother told me he had decided to update our subprime-player calculation routines.

The subprime algorithms were functionality we'd had in our VR worlds since Dystopia Two. They found people in the real world who were of low value to the sponsors of our virtual worlds. We called them our 'losers'.

The in-game denizens who corresponded to our identified losers played a valuable role in our games: they remained at a normal level of attractiveness.

Almost every game denizen got a complementary and automatic looks-upgrade, but we'd found that a scattering of less lovely cast members was vital to believability - VR worlds didn't feel plausible if every single inhabitant was air-brushed.

The hard truth was, some of our denizens had to stay plain but, unfortunately, those unflattered folk didn't usually enjoy our worlds as much. We had to identify people we didn't mind losing as customers, and our subprime player routines worked out who to sacrifice.

It had been years since I'd written the code for the routines and we'd been meaning to revisit it for ages. In June, Nemo had finally got around to it. He wanted to know what the lives of our projected losers went on to look like in the analog world. Had we identified them correctly? Were they still in dead-end jobs? Or had we completely screwed up and half of them had become CEOs of MegaCorps?

Nemo spent weeks using the Panopticon to track down what had happened to our subprimes, but he found something strange. My brother realised he couldn't locate some of our losers anywhere in the Panopticon nations.

His first thought was, were they dead? Was the subprime algorithm actually spotting potential suicide victims? It was possible. For voluntary deaths, nearly all Panopticon citizens made use of the services of an official executioner – an Undertaker like my friend Ray Creek. It was painless, tidy and completely free of charge – one of our highest rated public services.

Nemo cross-checked our loser lists against the public termination ones but none of our cohort appeared. Suicide didn't seem to be the explanation.

Perhaps we'd just identified unhealthy people who had died naturally? Nemo ran an analysis across all our losers worldwide and found most of them were alive, kicking and completely fine. They were as healthy as average.

Nemo narrowed his search down to 18 unexplained missing people. They had all lived in London and had vanished from the Panopticon sometime in the past two years, although most had disappeared in the last three months.

If there was one thing Nemo had always loved it was a puzzle. He started to look at what the missing losers had in common - apart from living in the same city. They seemed much as our algorithms had predicted: in deadbeat jobs with no family, no money, and few friends. They all had eye-wateringly bad social credit scores and big debts - which had mysteriously been paid off just before their disappearance.

For each individual, my brother followed their final recorded day. For all of them, the last thing the Panopticon drones saw was our loser enter the city of Conundra.

PIES

Conundra, September 2054

"I'm starving. I refuse to tell you anything else until I've had something to eat," said Nemo.

I dragged my brother into the hotel dining room and ordered dinner. I was thinking furiously about what he'd told me. What had happened to the missing people? Were they still here somewhere? How could we find out?

Nemo finally pushed his empty plate away, "What we need to know," he said, "is what's happening to our losers? Are they walking into Conundra as people and coming out as pies?"

I stared down at the steak and kidney pudding in front of me and put down my fork.

"Waste not, want not," said Nemo. He grabbed my plate and started polishing off the remains of my dinner.

"Well, we know they're not re-entering the Panopticon as sausages," I watched my vanishing meal - I'd lost my appetite anyway, "because Conundra doesn't export any food. Of course, that doesn't tell us anything about what gets served in the city."

"If there was ever a good argument for the Panopticon Seal of Approval, that would be it," said Nemo, shoveling pastry into his mouth. "No, I don't think this is a Soylent Green reveal anyway. There's not enough profit in dodgy meat products - we've got plenty of pork for now." He paused, "By the way, Ray and Catterwade are doing some investigating for me back home."

"Does Laura know too?"

Nemo nodded.

Irritated as I was, I was glad he'd involved them. Nemo's judgment of people could be sorely lacking and there was a good chance he'd stop investigating a puzzle if it started to involve talking to actual humans. My brother normally preferred to outsource interpersonal interactions to me, but he seemed to have expanded that trusted circle to include my friends Ray and Catterwade. Laura he tended to avoid – she constantly told him off.

Ray Creek had plenty of experience "in crime" as he put it. I still didn't know if he had been a policeman or a criminal before the Hot Summer, but he was a trusted Panopticon citizen now. The taciturn Catterwade had been in the army in the '30s and she seemed happy to back Ray up if action was required.

"When I told Laura about the missing, I got the impression the Panopticon had already noticed the situation. These *are* their people we're talking about and the disappearance rate has gone up a lot in the past few months. Something must have shown up in their reports."

"We're not likely to spot a trend like this before they do – the Panopticon is swimming in citizen data."

Nemo nodded his head, "But, they have no jurisdiction here and there's no proof of any WorldGov crime. Panopticon citizens are perfectly at liberty to move to Conundra and never come back."

"If you told everyone else, I still don't understand why you kept me in the dark?"

He grinned, "Thousands of innocent holidaymakers blithely visit and leave Conundra every day. We reckoned it was safer for you to be as ignorant as them. You're hardly an Oscar-winning actor. We didn't think you were up to a secret mission. It was better that you maintained a low profile."

I wasn't sure how low my profile had been - I suspected I'd have done a better job with more information.

"Of course, this might all be completely innocent," I commented. "Our losers may just have emigrated. They could all happily be working in Conundra in a different set of dead-end jobs."

My brother nodded, "Yes they could. We need to do some digging around here and see if we can locate any of them." He grimaced, "Without Control and the Panopticon, that's going to take ages."

I thought for a moment, "Maybe we could get ourselves some help. Apparently, Conundra has a lot of Private Eyes."

♦ ♦ ♦

After dinner, we took our drinks back into the smaller bar and slumped into chairs by the window again. It was pitch dark outside - the city clearly maintained the blackout. *That must be a WorldGov rule rather than a Panopticon suggestion*, I thought.

"I'm still thinking about my Conundran storyline - the woman who was shot," I mused, taking a swig of my Scotch. "There's something odd about it. I wonder if it's related to our mystery."

"I booked you some romantic nonsense," dismissed Nemo. "That story's a waste of your time. Drop it like a stone."

"So, that wasn't an admin mistake? What on earth made you buy a holiday romance for me?"

"Laura reckoned you needed a," he mimicked her voice, "'nice relaxing break'."

I shook my head in disgust.

"I know," Nemo agreed, "she made me sign you up for a week of candlelit dinners and lost treasure maps. How's that working out? Met anyone dreamy?" he mimed sticking two fingers down his throat.

"I think they messed that up somehow. At least, they didn't try very hard to set me up with anyone." I paused, "I told you, I stumbled on a murderous conspiracy instead. I'm not sure if it's real or not."

"It's obviously not real, that's the point of this place. Don't be such a rube." Nemo looked thoughtful, "They're doing a surprisingly decent job of putting it across though if even you're wondering." He waved his hand, "Forget it! We've got bigger fish to fry. My actual whodunit is a lot more important than your fake one."

I wasn't convinced my little brother was right. My gut told me there was more to the shot woman than he believed. Nonetheless, I was happy to stick to one crime at a time. There was no point arguing about it.

I switched my attention back to the problem he'd just presented. "You had planned to let me stay here for a week, get an unbiased feel for the place, and fill you in on the setup?"

He nodded.

I continued, "And you were making progress outside with access to Control and the Panopticon?"

He nodded again.

"So, why the hell have you turned up here after only 24 hours?"

"Something has happened and I reckoned you needed to know about it. Coming here in person was the only way to get in touch with you." He grimaced, "A new loser has disappeared and it was an old friend of yours."

I stared blankly.

"Yesterday, the real version of your greasy barman from the Utopia Five sim was on the same train to Conundra as you. I checked this morning - his debts have all been paid off."

GOGGLES

Conundra, September 2054

To say the greasy barman was a friend of mine was a stretch on Nemo's part - after all, I'd only met one of his digital versions. Nonetheless, Nemo was right - I did want to know about him arriving here. If the greasy barman or anyone else was in danger because of us we'd need to do everything possible to rescue them. Of course, it wasn't clear yet if our losers actually needed rescuing.

I started to think about how we could find this guy. At least, I thought, we'd recognise his un-airbrushed face if we saw it.

"Hand me your goggles," said Nemo, suddenly. "Have you been wearing them?"

I passed them over, "Of course, they are part of my costume."

He turned them around in his hands, "Good. I reckoned you would," he glanced up at me, "and have you met the Warlock yet?"

I shook my head, "Apparently, you do that on your last day."

"Damn. That guy has been avoiding photographs for years. It's suspicious." Nemo frowned in frustration.

I had wondered if the goggles were some kind of recording device. Those were strictly forbidden in Conundra, but I couldn't see my little brother letting that worry him - especially as I was the one wearing them.

"I assume they're an offline video camera?"

Nemo nodded, "We need to know more about the Warlock's involvement. For that, we need an image of him we can follow in Control."

He grasped his pipe firmly and stared off into the middle distance. He was really getting into his

Victorian detective character. I wondered if I'd ever get him out of that cape.

"We need to know who the Warlock was before Conundra and what he gets up to in the Panopticon nations, *if* he ever leaves the city. I was counting on you seeing him in person – the goggles would have finally caught him on camera."

My brother touched the sovereign ring he was wearing on his left hand to the steampunk spectacles and continued, "The goggles contain a high-definition video camera. The battery drain is minimal – they should have lasted your full week without recharging. They will have recorded footage of everything you've seen so far even if you didn't know you'd seen it." He grinned and wiggled his fingers, "That's your data downloaded. It's just a shame we still don't have any film of our mystery man."

Something occurred to me, "Hang on, I have seen something." I told Nemo about the photograph hanging on the wall of the Council offices: the picture of Concordia Clarke, Head of Mystery and Intrigue, and the Warlock. "It was old – from about 15 years ago – but it might be clear enough."

"Great, we should be able to use that."

Nemo rotated the front of the left-hand lens and handed the goggles back. "There, now they're in active mode. They're still offline, of course."

I put them back on, "What does active mode do?"

"The option to switch to IR filters. Plus telescopic sighting, head-up display and some useful image processing based on that work you did six months ago to your suit visor." Nemo looked smug, "Your code was a half-decent idea, but it could have been implemented way better so that's what I did. These goggles home in on every face within the extended range, record it and automatically scan for dupes - people you've seen multiple times. Be careful though, active mode does more real-time processing so it'll drain your batteries faster. If you do need to recharge, you can do it here," he pointed to a small socket on the inside of the arm. "You can return it to passive mode by twisting the lens back again."

I decided to try it out. I looked out through the double bar doors into the main hotel lobby. Through my lenses, Phyllida was now outlined in red and tagged with her name.

"You're sure it's offline?" I asked.

"D'uh," he replied, rolling his eyes.

If they weren't online, the goggles must include a microphone and audio processing, I thought. They must have picked up Phyllida Fogg's name when I spoke to her earlier and tagged her image. I was impressed - though I was hardly going to admit that to my annoying little brother.

A few of the other guests were also outlined. When I focused on them, the head-up display told me I'd seen them several times before at the current location. I hadn't spoken to them so they weren't name-tagged yet. *These goggles could be very useful*, I thought. *It's brilliant work.*

"They're OK, I suppose," I said to Nemo, dismissively.

I looked out of the window into the night, wondering how well the IR would work from inside a lit environment. Suddenly, an alert went off. The head-up display highlighted a person in the distance whose outline immediately started strobing. I peered at the flashing silhouette and the goggles automatically zoomed in and went to the IR view. *This really is impressive*, I thought.

The on-lens screen flashed up a message. According to my goggles, I'd encountered this person three times in the past 36 hours. I moved my gaze to the popup, which expanded. The screen informed me the same individual had been watching me from a crowd that afternoon - an encounter I hadn't noticed but my eyewear clearly had. I continued scrolling down. That morning, they had been outside the Leviathan bar. *Aha*, I thought, *my mysterious watcher*. I kept reading. Finally, the previous evening I'd seen the same sinister figure slip back into Conundra station after the cloud-haired woman was shot.

CHASE

*Conundra, September
2054*

Leaping to my feet, I dashed out of the hotel. When I reached the outside, I stopped briefly for the goggles to relocate my mysterious shadow. The glasses homed in on the figure's location and an AR overlay told me the fastest running route to get there. Nemo really had done a good job with this device. I took off, grinning. This time, I would be a lot harder to escape.

I saw the individual glance up in surprise and take off. After a hundred yards, they slid behind a large pillar box. Even without my IR goggles, I scornfully doubted whether such an obvious move would have fooled me. Then I realised it probably had when they'd lost me that morning so I shouldn't scoff at their camouflage skills. Maybe the Panopticon had made us all lightweights in the hide-and-seek department? I understood that game was a lot less popular than it used to be - after all, Deus would just tell you where everyone was.

As I sprinted towards the hiding place, I wondered why anyone would be following me - especially from the first moment I arrived. Perhaps it was part of my story? I thought that was supposed to be a romance though, why would I need a tail?

I ran around the pillar and confronted a six-foot tall figure in a long, camel-coloured trench coat, "Who the hell are you and why are you watching me!" I demanded.

At that moment, it occurred to me there was another logical reason why the person who I'd just cornered in a lonely street, whilst unarmed and unarmoured, might be following me. Perhaps it was because they'd shot someone and I was the only witness.

Shit, I thought.

PIP

*Conundra, September
2054*

The tall figure in front of me stood up straight, pulled off her hat and shook out a curly bob.

"Damn! I knew you'd catch me eventually. A single-person tail never works – it's way too obvious." She dug around in the pocket of her raincoat, removing a handkerchief, a pen and several scraps of paper before finally locating a small, cream card. She handed it to me saying, "The name's Marlowe, P.I."

The card said: Pip Marlowe, Private Investigator, 43 Humphrey Street. I turned it over to read the motto on the back, 'Don't *be* a Dick – Hire One'

"Pip Marlowe?" I said.

"You need a P.I. pseudonym in this place or you don't get any work," she said, apologetically.

"OK," I laughed, "I'll buy you're an investigator but why are you following me?"

"The Panopticon asked me to watch you." Pip paused, "Don't you realise? Conundra is a dangerous place!"

EGGS

Conundra, September 2054

The next morning at breakfast, Nemo pointedly bashed in the top of his egg with a teaspoon.

"That could have been your head last night at the hands of some goon in the pay of the Warlock. You don't have your suit here or any weapons. Chasing after bad guys is a pretty idiotic move," he paused, "even for you."

I couldn't argue. Annoying as he was, in this case my little brother was right. Having said that, it wasn't like we had any alternative – we didn't have any other backup.

Nemo caught my expression, "Ray and Catterwade arrive tonight."

"With their usual equipment?"

He nodded.

I was relieved. It was the logical move once Nemo realised we might have to stage a rescue attempt on our loser. He must have set it up before he left the Panopticon.

"We'll want to grab the greasy barman quickly once Ray and Catterwade get here," I stated. "The Conundran Council is likely to spot the pair of them fast because they're not going to look like holidaymakers. Especially if Catterwade brings her kit."

I looked at my pocket watch, "By the way, I've arranged for us to meet Pip Marlowe at 6:30 a.m. Her office is near the station. There's something I need her to do for us." I had been intending to hire a P.I. but we might as well use the one that had fallen into our laps.

"Good," said Nemo. "Afterwards, can we grab a train and get far enough out of the city to connect to the net. I want to track down that Warlock photo. We don't know if he's behind this yet, but I'd bet on it."

"How about Edge City," I proposed.

"Great, while we're there, we can talk to the Graeae."

Yuck, I grimaced to myself, *The Graeae are so creepy - but they do have cool stuff.*

Despite the Graeae, Edge City suited me fine - there was a package there I wanted to collect.

THE P.I.

Conundra, September 2054

It took half an hour to walk to P.I. Marlowe's place. *The whole Nostalgia Zone looks like an Edward Hopper painting,* I thought. *Nighthawks.* Someday I'd come back and hang out in an empty diner after dark. First up, murderous conspiracies didn't defeat themselves.

We finally found her office. It had a small shopfront sandwiched between a closed laundromat and a deserted cafe. Pip Marlowe spotted us peering through the grimy windows, waved us inside, and handed us two mugs of milky tea.

"You made it through the night. Good stuff!" she observed. I wasn't sure if she was serious.

"Welcome," she continued, "to the secret embassy of the Panopticon."

I looked around at the peeling paint and the heavily-dented Formica table she was perched on. I didn't think much of the place.

"I," she declared, "am the Panopticon's woman in Conundra."

"A spy?" Nemo asked, "Do the Conundrans know about you?"

"No. At least, we don't think so. They do have eyes and ears everywhere though, so who knows? Whatever," she grinned, "they seem to leave me alone."

"It's not like you're enemies," Nemo observed. "Conundra and the Panopticon are WorldGov signatories. You both follow all the global laws."

"True," replied Pip, "we've just never established formal relations. You could say I'm the unofficial ambassador."

"Who works as a private detective?" I asked.

"Conundra has a lot of Private Eyes," Marlowe retorted. "What better cover could I have?"

She has a point, I thought. I wondered if the city's P.I. services only got used by visitors or, given the lack of Panopticon cameras and the hordes of cheap detectives, the subjects of Conundra paid for constant tails on one another.

"Since our drones can't see this place I understand why the Panopticon wants someone keeping a physical eye on it, but it seems pretty harmless to me. Why all the sneaking around?" I asked.

"Conundra is not as benign as it appears," Pip replied, pursing her lips. "We've been investigating the state for a while." She took a sip from her mug, "A lot of our citizens have disappeared into the city recently and never been heard from again." Pip Marlowe shook her head, "No matter what the Conundran council says, we don't believe they've all stayed willingly. This week, I finally got my first decent lead but that turned into a dead end." The P.I. glowered at me for some reason. "The trouble is, thousands of Panopticon visitors arrive every week. We don't know which citizen will go missing and by the time we know that someone has, the trail has gone cold. I'm getting nowhere!"

Nemo and I exchanged a look. It sounded like Pip Marlowe and the Panopticon were working on the same case as us.

Pip continued, "We're limited in what we can do. Panopticon citizens are entitled to emigrate to Conundra. None of the missing folk had any friends or family and so no one has asked WorldGov to investigate. We've had to dig around quietly." She grimaced, "We've been forced to do this old school. Door-to-door and face-to-face. In other words, spadework."

"I still don't understand why you were tailing me?" I said. "I've only just arrived, I couldn't know anything yet."

Her eyes widened, "Isn't it obvious? The Panopticon assembly was worried about you going missing too. We watch anyone on our critical individuals list that comes to Conundra. It hardly ever happens - you folk never take a vacation - and now two of you!" she shook her head.

She continued, "As soon as the name Lee Sands was flagged up, we had a word with your

Panopticon minder. She tried to make sure you'd have a dull holiday but warned us you might still get into trouble. She told us to tail you from the moment you stepped off the train. She was right – you ran straight into that shooting."

Marlowe gave an annoyed laugh, "That was the best lead I'd got all year and I had to leave it to bodyguard you safely to your hotel."

I wondered what she meant about my minder.

She sighed, "I didn't even get a good look at the victim and by the time I got back, the scene was so clean I could have performed open heart surgery in that alley. Whoever killed the woman knew what they were doing."

"It really was a murder!" I exclaimed.

"Of course it was! They fired a bloody bullet right at you. It only missed you by inches," she said, shaking her head as if I was a complete fool, which I clearly was. "I've been shadowing you ever since in case they tried to finish the job. As far as they knew, you were the only witness."

I thought about the woman collapsing in front of me. How could I have been such an idiot! Maybe I could have helped her! *Or got myself shot too*, I thought.

"I think we can help you out on the victim ID." I took off my goggles, switched them into active mode, and located the footage from the shooting. "Maybe you can get something from this?" I said, handing her the device.

Pip peered at the recording, "This is great!"

She opened a cupboard, pulled out an old printer and, from a freeze frame, ran off a handful of photographs of the murdered woman.

"Are you allowed that?" I asked, pointing at the presumably renegade tech. "Printers weren't invented in the 1950s."

"I'm the secret agent of a foreign power, plotting against the state." Pip shrugged, "Anachronistic printing is the least of my crimes."

TRAIN

*Between Conundra
and Edge City,
September 2054*

We finished our mugs of tea and handed Pip a snapshot that Nemo had brought with him of our new missing loser - the greasy barman from Utopia Five. "We suspect this guy is the next disappearing person. He only arrived here last night so his trail should still be warm."

"Can you also look into a woman called Katy, who works for the Council of Conundra?" I added, "It sounds like she's gone too." I frowned, "The Council must be involved somehow - Concordia Clarke definitely tried to put me off the scent." I paused, "Of course, she could have been acting under orders from someone else."

"Are you sure the shooting is related to the missing people?" Nemo questioned Marlowe, "You only ran across it because you were tailing Lee. It could just be a coincidence."

Pip looked skeptical, "How many murderous conspiracies are there likely to be in one place?"

That, I thought, was a good question.

◆ ◆ ◆

Nemo and I walked from Marlowe's office to the station. We'd agreed to meet up with her at the hotel that evening to go over whatever she'd found out. In the meantime, we couldn't track down the Warlock from here. We needed the net.

Wireless and mobile signals were blocked across the city. We'd have to go beyond the borders of the state before we could get online. If we only needed net access we could have just taken the train to the nearest town in the Panopticon, but I wanted something more. I looked at the board as we entered the terminus. There was a departure to Edge City in 25 minutes. I guessed it would be quiet. No one went there in the flesh if they could avold it.

Edge City was a seaport roughly twenty miles northeast of Conundra. It was one of the few Panopticon states that welcomed folk who wanted to be a little more creative with technology – at least, more creative than the average citizen was comfortable with.

Nemo loved the place but it wasn't really to my taste. It had been years since I'd last visited in person, although if I needed imaginative tech I'd often get it built there.

I sighed. I knew Nemo was right. If we were going to the city we'd both have to pay our respects to the Graeae – they'd know we were there as soon as our train arrived. *Toughen up,* I thought, *we might need their help with our research.* I wondered what they'd ask for in return and flinched.

The Edge City train pulled up and I looked along the platform. No one else was getting on, so we weren't being followed. *Though we could be being watched,* I thought, and gazed at two Roman centurions who were chatting together by the ticket office. They didn't look familiar but, if I was being honest, one centurion looked much like another to me.

Was I being paranoid? Our conversation with Pip Marlowe had made me nervous about hanging out in Conundra with no protection. I wondered if Pip could look after herself. She'd obviously survived up until now. I frowned and hoped that wasn't only because of the dearth of clues she'd managed to uncover. Now she had a photo of the next victim she might be more worthy of malign attention.

♦ ♦ ♦

Our train carriage was almost empty. We sat on either side of a table by the window and my brother looked me up and down, "I reckon you can get away with wearing that costume in Edge," he said, "but I'd prefer to make a better impression."

"Don't worry," I replied, "I've got something being built there at the moment. I'll pick it up on our way in. Now that I know more about Conundra, I think I want it with me," I grinned, "and I'm sure I can impress your friends."

Nemo sniffed. He stared in disgust at the low-res screen built into the tabletop in front of us and then patted all his cape pockets.

"Can I borrow your goggles?" he said. "I need a good display that's a little more discreet."

I could see it wasn't the subtlest plan to start investigating the Warlock on a public device. Everything displayed on that screen would certainly be recorded and it might throw up an alert to the Conundran Council.

"Here. Can you confirm Pip's story while you're at it? Sounds like Laura should know about her."

He nodded, grabbed the glasses, and waited a few minutes for the train to hit the Panopticon border. I guessed he'd confirm safe net access with Deus and then get to work.

Once we had left the city I sighed with relief, put in my earpiece for the first time in 36 hours, and stared out the window. We were passing fields full of human and drone activity. Our route to Edge City would take us through one corner of the eastern grass farms, which provided almost a quarter of the protein for London. Deus informed me that local irrigation projects were in full progress. Through the train window, I could see crowds of people on foot, carrying tools.

"They're going to the dig sites," said Deus, guessing my thoughts as the chatbot often did.

If I was wearing my goggles, I knew in augmented reality I'd see bright indigo halos around the groups. Omniscience Industries had rolled out their new AR Aura feature about three months ago and the irrigation projects were tough, important work - highly valued by Kirby and the Panopticon. The workers' community value scores would be sky high. They'd have great auras.

I thought about Dave the Celt. Since he worked on one of the irrigation schemes, in the Panopticon he must have an aura like that. His halo obviously hadn't come with him to Conundra and without any visor tech in the city there was no AR to see auras with anyway. He must have badly wanted to visit Conundra to give up that social status, I thought, even for a few days.

I glanced down at my own hand, which was mundane-looking without contacts or a visor. With my social scores, I glowed faintly green in AR. I was proud of that. I was a decent member of society, although not as highly valued as the agriworkers, of course. Writing computer games wasn't a particularly worthy occupation even if it was lucrative.

I looked at my brother. In AR he was a no-glower and a reminder that, no matter how rich you are, your gold pieces don't count towards your community value scores. Not that Nemo cared about his lack of a halo. As if sensing my thoughts, he looked up and grinned.

I thought about the grass farms that the workers were irrigating. Nearly a decade ago, we'd realised it was a good way to sequester carbon and restore our topsoil. The idea wasn't new; a few folk had been grass farming way before '36. It never caught on back then because it was innately manual and hard to industrialise. Once we had less fuel, everything became labour intensive so grass farming didn't seem as bad - all agriwork required more humans.

The farms worked using small pastures and fast rotation of crops and animals. They usually cycled grass, cows and chickens. The idea was you would let a grass field grow to waist height, to encourage deep roots, and then you brought in cows.

In a single day, the herd would eat all your grass and shit generously over your field. That evening, you'd move your cows out, and something interesting would happen. Underground, the grass roots would die back and leave a bunch of carbon sequestered in the soil. At the same time, maggots would start to grow in the manure.

A few days later, you'd release your chickens. They'd have what can only be described as a field day eating the maggots.

It was one of the best ways to provide food for the populace: dairy, eggs, chicken, and meat – and the farmer now had a well-fertilised field, ready for the grass to regrow. Plenty of carbon had been sequestered and the topsoil was a little thicker. After a few years, the soil would support crops again.

It was a system that transformed carbon in the air back into better soil in the ground with fat and protein production as a side benefit. The milk and eggs were dried in situ with huge solar dehydrators, then transported to local cities. We even got the occasional steak, though most of the fresh meat went to the on-site agriworkers.

Of course, we couldn't live on grass alone. Oats, pulses, wheat flour and potatoes came into London from all over Britain in the autonomous lorry convoys, along with fruit from the land that wasn't irrigated yet: apples from the North, grapes and olives from the South coast. The whole system would be pretty stable if it wasn't for the ongoing storms. The constant repairs were exhausting.

As we passed a large building on our left, Deus informed me a slaughterhouse was within sight. I brought up the public screen on the table in front of me and performed my duty by looking in. As a citizen, it was our shared responsibility to verify the way the animals we ate were killed. I'd read that before the Seal inhumane stuff had happened behind closed doors. I shook my head over pre-Panopticon society - didn't they realise the only way to police the supply chain was if every citizen did it?

The slaughterhouse was clean and the animals looked blissfully unaware of their impending doom, so I gave the place a good rating. That would help them maintain their Seal. In theory, you didn't need the Seal to sell meat but, as the Conundrans had found out, without it no right-minded Panopticoner would eat your stuff. People would have to be crazy or starving to buy food that wasn't observable and we tried to make sure no one was that desperate. It occurred to me I'd been eating meat in Conundra without a Seal. I resolved to switch to vegetarian when I got back there.

"Lee," said the Deus chatbot conversationally through my earpiece, "the farmer needs a loan of 10,000 Sols to fund an upgrade to that slaughterhouse. The expected rate of return is 1%. He has a credit worthiness score of 98% – excellent."

"Fine," I said. "Transfer it from my account." I'd noticed Deus and the local populace were very hand-in-glove these days. And that gloved hand often seemed to be in my pocket. Still, with a credit rating like that the farmer would be good for it.

I turned back to Nemo, who was taking off my steampunk goggles. "I've spoken to the Graeae," he said. "They have the Warlock photo now. They'll clean it up and see what they can find out."

◆ ◆ ◆

"If those missing people are dead," I said, staring out of the window, "it will be our fault."

"We didn't put a gun to their heads and pull the trigger." Nemo protested.

"Maybe not, but we certainly painted on a target. You heard Pip; they were people who no one would miss; people who didn't matter. That's what our algorithms identified: potential victims. Then we put the data out there in public for anyone to see. We created an antisocial credit system."

"But we didn't mean to."

"It's worse than that. It never occurred to us." I frowned, "I'm fully aware it was all my idea."

I thought about something Alex Lidenbrock had said to me about Kant.

"I reckon I treated those people as means not ends: they were a way to improve our World aesthetics without hitting our sponsorships. I didn't actually think about them at all. They were like those characters in a book that are only there to serve the plot," I said.

"I hate that," whispered my brother, shaking his head, "but we *are* a business not a charity and we can't predict everything."

It occurred to me that, despite his protests, Nemo was the one who'd done the right thing. He'd followed up on the folk we'd tagged as losers. We should have done it sooner. Although, I mused, until there were a significant number of disappearances we probably wouldn't have noticed anyway - that was the problem with statistical analysis.

"We need to fix this. Can we turn off the feature immediately? Work out how to replace it later?"

He nodded, "It'll cost us users."

"Yeah, maybe a conscience has become my new expensive hobby."

I looked keenly at Nemo, "So, we're assuming the losers are disappearing because our VR Worlds imply no one would miss them."

"Yep. Someone has been prowling around virtual London in one of our games, looking for un-airbrushed folk as potential victims - people they can take without raising too much attention," he agreed.

"We suspect our perp is associated with the Conundran Council. We also know they've stepped up their activity in the last few months – that's why the Panopticon has suddenly noticed. The first question is, why are they doing it?" I thought for a moment. "It could be a lone psychopath?"

Nemo pondered that, "Could be, but it smells more like a conspiracy to me. I don't like the way the Warlock is so shadowy. Keeping your picture secret these days is hard. Plus: bushy white hair, eyebrows and a mustache?"

"An obvious disguise?"

"Sounds like it to me."

I thought about the complete ban on recording devices in the city. "So, our next question," I mused, "is does the Warlock even exist?"

SCORES

London, 2043

B ack in the early days of our games, we'd toyed with a lot of business models. Potentially, one of the most lucrative was individual ratings. Deus, the ubiquitous chatbot of Omniscience Industries, had grabbed an early lead on social scores but we had capabilities it didn't. I reckoned we could beat God when it came to judging people.

Social credit scores had been around since well before '36. The idea was to rank people or firms on stuff like how popular or competent they were. Loads of the early social media companies scored folk based on how many friends or fans they had and businesses were rated on customer reviews. The whole thing was intrusive but useful and people were willing to trade their own privacy for better data on everyone else. It was the same pact we made over the Panopticon.

Even before the Panopticon went live in 2025, ratings – trust data - had been an earner for businesses for years. Scores were generally limited in scope and somewhat transparent: you could often confirm where they came from by counting followers or reading reviews yourself. That's not to say they were never gamed - as I mentioned, scores were big business so some people would always cheat.

Before the Panopticon, the point of it all was usually to make money. Ratings sites took an advertising fee or maybe a cut of the sales price. Retailers sold more of products that had good 'star' counts.

Some Governments used social scores to encourage the behaviour they wanted and discourage the stuff they didn't like: shaming people for jaywalking or paying bills late. That could get a bit authoritarian - like not letting you travel by train if you didn't recycle your coffee cups - but was that wrong? The Hot Summer had made us realise there were limits to liberty.

By the early 20's, there were hundreds of businesses that rated people on their trustworthiness for niche activities like cat-sitting or flapjack-cooking or whatever. I guess they were a sign of the Panopticon-to-come. Laura told me the Panopticon had thought about providing social ratings themselves, but decided to leave it to the commercial sector. Kirby Cross was happy to step in and, by 2030, all the most popular ratings were from Deus.

For nearly sixty years, search engines had been ranking information. Since the Deus chatbot was kind of a search engine for humans, it made sense for it to start ranking people. It didn't surprise me that Kirby Cross loved the idea of scoring folk on how good they were - he definitely had a God complex and weighing souls was within his self-appointed brand. Deus literally became critical infrastructure.

At least Kirby Cross was self-aware. Unlike a real God - arbitrary and capricious - he made sure anyone could see anything that contributed to an individual's scores and consider them for themselves. The judgment of Deus was transparent and you always had a right of challenge. Even if you lost your soul appeal, you could write a statement in your own defense so people could assess for themselves your gibbering self-justifications. Kirby was tough – but he was fair.

Whether Deus's scores did anything worse than make people look askance at you in the dentist's waiting room depended on the state you were in. Some populations were more authoritarian than others and individual states had a lot of discretion from WorldGov – the only thing they had to do was provide you with health, food, shelter, and access to WorldGov infrastructure.

Before Nemo's and my first Dystopia game took off in '43, I'd been keen for us to try to create our own social scores. I reckoned we could do a better job than Deus, which relied heavily on asking for feedback on individuals from other people. Control, our full-world sim, could rate people automatically based on video analysis. Did other people smile at them? Did they drop litter? Did they hold doors open? I loved the idea. Nemo absolutely hated it and refused to add it to Control.

My brother intensely disliked scoring systems. In theory, scores were not the voice of God – they could be challenged and we could check someone's rating and see if we agreed with it. In reality, very few of us actually did that. Mostly, we blindly accepted what Deus - or ultimately Kirby Cross - told us to think.

I had to admit, 90% of the time I was too busy or lazy to question Deus's judgment and sometimes stories were "too good to check". There was also a big difference between the people who understood how tech like Deus and Control worked and those who didn't. Folk who blindly accepted what they were told, for whatever reason, could still be manipulated. That definitely included me sometimes.

The Panopticon could punish manipulators when they spotted them but we couldn't just rely on that. I suspected keeping yourself educated enough to make good judgments based on Panopticon data was part of your civic duty. I kept trying to persuade Kirby to include tech-savviness in his community value scores but he reckoned we'd need to fund more adult education programs before we did that.

To be fair to Kirby, it was already one of Deus' definitions of good citizenship that you got involved and reviewed things. If you took too many shortcuts you got demerits. I got plenty of them myself. If I was busy, I often skipped my legislation review duties and that was an automatic

Panopticon fine plus a hit on my community scores. The fines were wealth-based so mine were steep. That was the correct thing to do, I reckoned. A fixed fine would mean doing something illegal would be less bad for me than for most other people and that was no way to run a society.

Not that variable fines meant we lived in some kind of egalitarian utopia - the impact of a bad social score was way less for rich folk. Nemo certainly didn't care about his score. If people charged him more because they thought he was less trustworthy, he could afford to take the hit. Plus, he didn't need to worry about loans and if strangers wouldn't speak to him in pubs he was completely fine with that.

I had good social scores and Panopticon citizens always chatted to me. Although, I didn't have any scores in Conundra and people there talked to me anyway. That made me wonder how much difference the ratings really made?

Humans are designed to estimate other people's trustworthiness. In Conundra, I thought, that was still based on surface appearances. If we were going to make judgments, surely it was better to go on someone's past behaviour, like in the

Panopticon, rather than what they looked like right now, like in Conundra?

I knew Nemo would say, "Why should a past mistake hang over me in my scores forever?" I tended to think, if you'd done something wrong your right to leave that behind didn't trump my right to know about it. The real problem was who defined what 'something wrong' meant? Especially since most people just accepted Deus' score and that was primarily Kirby Cross's opinion. How could that be right? Should we have a separate legal system for social scores? Or even make it religious and have churches do it?

Maybe Deus has it right, I thought. At least Kirby published his rules about civic and moral duties. You knew what you needed to do to comply. His rules had become enshrined in society.

I frowned. Was Alex Lidenbrock right? Had we let Kirby Cross become the Panopticon's King?

THE FAN

Between Conundra
and Edge City,
September 2054

My pocket watch told me we were still a few minutes out of Edge City when I noticed a guy in his twenties at the far end of the carriage was staring at me. *Time to work the community*, I thought.

I got up, walked down to his seat, stopped, and stretched out my hand, "Lee Sands. Pleased to meet you."

"I know! I know!" he squeaked, "I'm Dan, Dan Richards! Actually, we've met!"

Have we? I thought. He didn't look familiar.

"Kind of met anyway," he smiled shyly, "I battle velociraptors with you every day!" he paused in embarrassment. "I know that's not the same."

I smiled. This was a conversation I had a lot.

From the start, in our VR Worlds Nemo and I knew we'd need some star denizens – characters our players would want to fight alongside. We needed the real world counterparts of those denizens to chat to players they met and be our ambassadors. Give interviews. All that stuff.

In the early days, we couldn't afford to pay anyone to do that so the obvious job candidates were Nemo or me. My brother flatly refused – he hated talking to strangers. In the past he'd tried to make sure no one knew what he looked like or even how his denizens might be found. For a while, I'd reckoned the only player that could get anywhere near his virtual selves was me.

As the Panopticon data got better, hiding had become impossible. *I guess*, I thought, *that's why he knows how difficult staying invisible would've been for the Warlock.* I suspected it would be easier if you holed yourself up as the supreme leader of your own city with complete control over the cameras and a ban on all personal recording equipment.

Nemo had a holiday home. That wasn't quite the same.

So, I would have to be the star. To make me into a high profile denizen, Nemo had tweaked reality around my characters in the Dystopias. He didn't do anything that broke the laws of physics, obviously, but my VR versions had implausible luck: the bad luck to always be in the centre of the action, and the astonishing good luck to stay alive while there. If you met a version of me in a game you'd think <I> had God in my back pocket – because <I> did. If my denizens didn't have Nemo manipulating the world around them, they wouldn't be interesting enough.

A few years ago, we started hiring good players to be VIP denizens too. They couldn't affect their alter-egos in the games – Nemo handled raising their profile there – they just had to stay current with their VR selves' exploits and chat in person and online to other players. It was a big part of our games community. The stars didn't need to be heroic types – Nemo made sure their denizens found top-of-the-range exoskeletons and weaponry and, of course, had a lot of luck.

I smiled at Dan and quickly cast my mind through our games to work out which one he was talking about - fighting dinosaurs was a popular pastime for my denizens. "Dystopia 16, 25 or 32?" I asked.

"25," he replied enthusiastically.

"Ah yes. 'Dystopia 25: In Space, No One Can Hear You Splat'. It's one of my favourites. Armoured velociraptors have got free on Moonbase Four and eaten the entire military high command," I paused. "It was a lucky break Sergeant Lee Sands was in the shower when the dinos broke out. Genetically engineered superlizards hate anti-dandruff shampoo. Thank Deus I always use it."

Dan nodded enthusiastically.

"It's a good Dystopia," I continued, then shook my head ruefully. "Those 'raptors are tough. I hope you haven't been eaten too often? 187 times? Well, Sergeant Sands appreciates your persistence, soldier."

I gave him the salute of the EDF: the Extraplanetary Defense Force. "Keep a 360!" I barked.

"Roger!!" he replied, returning the salute and looking ecstatic.

Nemo gave me a smug look – he was pleased with Dystopia 25. I thought it was a bit hackneyed. In my opinion, once we had dinosaurs, upping the stakes on location for new games was just cheap. Although, admittedly, always a good earner.

I noticed the train was grinding to a halt. A voice came over the speaker system. Cows had apparently wandered onto the line and we would be here some time. I shrugged and sat down with Dan. I was always happy to discuss battle tactics and there was nothing we could do about the bovine invasion. At least they were unlikely to be armed, I thought, this wasn't Dystopia 9.

EDGE

Edge City, September 2054

O ur train only got held up for twenty minutes. I finally shook hands with Dan the fan and joined Nemo on the platform.

"Another happy user?" he asked.

"Of course," I grinned, "I enjoyed that - and he's re-broadcasting the conversation on community channels right now. It should boost our ratings."

I looked around us. I'd been to Edge City several times before but it remained startling every visit. The Edge, as residents called the place, was part of the Panopticon nations just like London. I looked up into the sky and saw the familiar covering of drones. Everything here was recorded for everyone to see and I had full access to the net, Deus and our own Control sim. It was just like home.

The only difference in Edge City was one of attitude. Everyone here was watched, but absolutely no one cared. All the social credit systems were completely ignored in Edge City, which gave it an odd feeling of lawlessness mixed with a kind of reckless freedom. It was Nemo's kind of place.

One of the things some people worry about in the Panopticon states is that the general public can be disapproving of radical tech - they take a while to get used to new ideas. In the early days, the average Earthling-in-the-street was skeptical about organ transplants, stem cell research and nuclear power. New ideas can be messy to start with. They take a while to get into a stable, acceptable state and people are suspicious until then. Folk have also got less trusting of technology since the Hot Summer. Scientists and engineers who work on groundbreaking stuff can end up with low social ratings even if their discoveries become popular eventually.

Edge City was a place you could work on projects without worrying about the public quite so much. The other residents wouldn't shun you just because you had social scores even lower than my brother's. I didn't like to admit it to Nemo, but I could see the logic of Edge City. We still needed to develop new tech and the general population could be a dead hand stopping progress. There was a tricky balance between allowing the public to kill bad science without letting them put the brakes on everything.

The Edge citizens on the station platform were fairly typical. For a moment, I had thought I fitted in well in my steampunk goggles - about half the crowd seemed to be wearing them. On closer inspection, I realised I was the only person whose eyewear wasn't attached permanently to their face. I remembered that Edge City was always like a Borg convention.

"I'm surprised you never had anything welded on," I said to Nemo.

He winked, "I had my right ulna replaced with memory plastic this year," he tapped his arm smugly. "It's usually connected to my contacts - full recording and replay. Everything your goggles do but a little more discreet."

That was OK, I supposed. I preferred my suit. Thinking of which, "What time is our appointment with the Graeae? There's something I need to pick up first."

Nemo checked his watch, "An hour. Meet there? I want to check on our yard while we're here."

I knew Nemo couldn't spend any time in this city without visiting his favourite factory. My brother had been obsessed with submarines since he was a kid. That was how he'd got his nickname. It was also how we got so involved with the formation of Edge City. The place was founded on the site of what had once been Britain's largest container port. Of course, the Hot Summer had ended that.

Like cars, in '38 WorldGov had classified carbon-powered cargo and transport ships as threats to the remainder of humanity and severely restricted them. Only a handful of the cleanest stayed in service and only for high priority goods - mostly large scale emergency relief. WorldGov had bankrolled projects to refit ports for sail-powered trading. Places like Edge City, with its relatively safe harbours and access to all of Britain and Europe by sea and rail, did very well. Or, at least, comparatively well.

Nemo and I were the prime backers in a couple of manufacturing outfits based in the city. My brother's favourite was a company that retrofitted defunct container ships, and some smaller vessels, with nuclear engines. Before the Summer, there were plenty of nuclear-powered ships: most aircraft carriers and subs were. So were a lot of icebreakers. That was how Nemo first got interested in the tech. Once diesel engines had been banned, nuclear was the obvious replacement.

Atomic Cargo Incorporated specialised in compact nuclear engines, designed and developed here in Edge City. They already had a big WorldGov contract and planned to operate out of the city's old port for a few years until the flooding got too bad. They were also working on designs for floating harbours, which were the only option given the speed of the sea rises. Atomic Cargo was Nemo's pet project, but I'd reviewed the numbers and they looked good. It was a solid, sensible investment and I reckoned we should turn a decent profit.

I watched my brother stride off to catch up with his nuclear engineers and checked my watch. I had 55 minutes until we met the Graeae. I reckoned I could just about make it.

NEW SUIT

Edge City, September
2054

When Nemo told me about my surprise holiday, he said, "Just relax! A break from tech won't kill you!" and I'd actually been grateful to the little weasel. I thought about how close a bullet had come to taking me out in a dark alley and shuddered.

I'd realised I should never go anywhere that banned suits and had decided to get my hands on a stealth exoskeleton before returning to Conundra. Fortunately, I always had some interesting tech under development in Edge City.

I hurried along a back street and stopped at a battered door on my right. It was covered with odd symbols and briefly reminded me of the Gothic zone in Conundra. As soon as I was within a foot of the entrance, it opened from the inside and I strode through. I knew the team would have been alerted to my presence as soon as I stepped off the train.

A gnomish woman with one arm and three metallic tentacles extending from her spine suddenly appeared, pulled me further inside and slammed the door.

"Hey Pam," I said apologetically, "sorry to drop in unannounced. I need an outfit for Conundra in a hurry. How's the new gear going?"

She had grabbed me with her organic arm, which was a relief – I could see two of her tentacles currently ended in pliers and those pinched, even through a suit. The other metallic arm terminated in something that looked like an egg whisk. I wondered what it was for.

Pam looked at me suspiciously. She and her team were artists and they didn't like being rushed or interrupted. I usually just handed them a large wad of cash and, eventually, they gave me back a work of art.

"I'm making my lunch," she snapped, slightly resentfully. "What do you want?"

"Speed, strength, bullet-proofness, and discretion," I replied, knowing Pam hated idle chit-chat.

"And what don't you need?"

"Computation, vacuum-rating," I thought for a moment, "or scuba."

"Combat-trained?" she asked.

"Highly."

"Given what you're wearing now, I assume we're talking discreet for the Steampunk Zone?"

I nodded.

She sucked her teeth, "Finished, I've got a super-lightweight, servo-assisted exoskeleton with hood. Combat-rated AA3 for hand-to-hand and gun work. We've paired it with six microdrones," she flashed open a compact case to show me half a dozen quadcopters. "These should fit in your pocket. The drones are just local area audio/video recon. No net connection and no firepower. Is that good enough?" I nodded. I expected Catterwade would bring some weaponry with her. She usually did.

"You can borrow a leather trench to cover the suit." Pam looked at my feet, "I see you're already wearing a pair of our boots. They'll do fine." She waved at my goggles with the whisk, "Were you keeping those? Because I think we can do better."

THE GRAEAE

Edge City, September 2054

"New outfit?" said Nemo. "What happened to the old goggles?"

"Don't worry, I transferred your code. These ones have better zoom - plus a few other features."

"They don't look as good," said Nemo.

My right lens flashed up that that was a lie. My new eyewear's facial analysis estimated a 92% chance my brother was experiencing extreme jealousy. I smiled. There was a 100% chance I was experiencing extreme smugness.

As planned, Nemo and I had met outside a huge warehouse next to the harbour. I looked up at the quadcopters and seagulls wheeling overhead. The doors to the building were open and hundreds of people were dashing in and out, while as many stood utterly still and stared into space.

"Who are we looking for?" I asked.

"Don't worry," Nemo replied, "they've known where we were the whole time we've been in the city. They'll find us."

A frozen woman about 10 feet away suddenly snapped to attention and looked straight at me. "The Sands of Time," she stated. "Come with me." She turned abruptly and marched through the entrance to the building. Nemo nodded and we followed.

I had never visited the British headquarters of the Graeae in person before. My dealings with the technocult had always been remote and usually via a lowly functionary. You might call the group eccentric – if understatement was your hobby. Frankly, I found even a video call with them difficult enough.

We walked into a huge, open warehouse full of even more people, all standing still with their eyes closed and an intense look of concentration on their faces. Every 30 seconds, they simultaneously moved into a new configuration. I had no idea what they were doing - for all I knew it was a dance class.

I assumed they were remotely connected in some way, but there was obviously some physical aspect to their system as well. I wondered if there was a useful technique here we could be learning from. Given how advanced some of the tech coming out of the Graeae cult was, I'd love to steal some of their processes.

I gazed up at the Panopticon drones hovering by the ceiling. I could clearly watch them anytime I wanted, but I suspected the visual component wouldn't be enough for me to tell what the hell was going on. I wondered if there was a way to join in short of joining the cult.

We strode across the hall and down a long, wide corridor on the far side.

"She's taking us to the throne room of the mighty tri-rulers," Nemo whispered.

I sighed. I'd dealt with egomaniacal executive boards before, "How do the mighty tri-rulers like to be addressed?"

"Your Visionarynesses."

Really? I thought. *Well, I've schmoozed worse.*

A pair of heavy wooden doors, painted gold and carved with two giant eyes, silently swung open in front of us. *Coming across as pretentious is clearly not something that keeps them awake at night*, I thought, and looked at Nemo.

"Throne room," he mouthed and walked through.

◆ ◆ ◆

On the other side of the doors, the room was completely unlit – the only light was coming from the opening behind us. My googles automatically switched to an IR overlay and I looked around.

It was apparent the wooden building had been extended over the harbor because the floor of the chamber was lapping seawater – apart from the small wooden platform we were currently standing on and another one in the middle of the space. On that, I could see the shapes of three seated people. I guessed we were supposed to reach them by walking across the narrow, unsteady-looking pontoon that joined the decks. The tide was low so, my goggles informed me, the pontoon was currently 3.4 metres below us. We'd have to climb a slimy metal ladder to reach it.

Damn, I thought, *I should have asked for that scuba functionality after all.*

Our guide indicated we should cross and then disappeared back through the door. I steeled myself and led the way. The water didn't bother me but I knew that what would greet us on the other side would require some self-control.

A few minutes later, we'd made it across the wobbling bridge and climbed onto the larger deck. In the dim light, I could see that in front of me were three figures on uncomfortable-looking stools. They were each dressed in a monk's robe with the cowl pulled up. Two had their eyes sewn shut, two had had their ears removed and two had their lips sealed. I looked closely, *press studs*, I guessed – you still had to eat. There seemed to be a Gorgon theme going on here, I thought. I could work with that. The cult leaders were obviously picked for being relatively presentable – I had been expecting worse.

The Graeae Collective was obsessed with minimizing extraneous senses to focus on digital inputs. *Personally, I'd have gone with dark glasses and earplugs*, I thought. That was probably why I wasn't the leader of a radical technocult.

I knew the Graeae usually had at least one implant that fed data into their visual or auditory cortices either directly from Panopticon drones or via a processing server. Many of them were connected to our Control VR sim or even one of our game worlds.

The tech for direct cortical input had been around a surprisingly long time. The same principle had been used for sixty years in the cochlear implants that provided a digital replacement for organic hearing.

The concept was interesting and I was tempted myself – the increase in neural data processing speed and bandwidth could be huge. With some Graeae implants, I could potentially think twice as fast as unenhanced humans; effectively doubling my conscious lifespan. The only problem was original, organic data feeds usually interfered with the Graeae's new ones. To get full benefit from their tech you had to make a choice and the earlier you made it the better. I swallowed, I wasn't about to ask for a tour of the nursery.

The Graeae Collective needed to be part of the Panopticon superstate for the data. Unfortunately, ordinary citizens tended to downvote them and their terrible social scores forced them to avoid mainstream society. The result was they mostly lived in Edge City or similar states with the other social outcasts. The public could be appallingly judgmental, I thought, especially if you were a tech-fetishizing weirdo with cognitive superpowers.

Nemo gave me a surreptitious nod and looked relieved. I guessed he'd recognised one of them.

I bowed deeply to each ruler in turn, "Your wise visionarynesses," I said, carefully. "We come to beg a boon."

"A booooon!" echoed the one in the centre, who was both ear and eyeless but did seem to have the only speaking part. I wondered what I looked like to him. *Like nothing I'd recognise as human*, I thought.

I realised I ought to spend a lot more time in this place. Internationally, the branches of the Graeae

Collective made up one of our largest groups of players, yet I didn't have any real understanding of how our games worked for them.

The gameplay must be good at the moment or they wouldn't all be fans, but I realised there was a risk we might make a seemingly innocuous change and break their user experience because we had so little understanding of what that experience was. Strange as they were, I thought, I desperately wanted to keep them happy as players – *they may all sleep on pallets in a warehouse,* I thought, *but this technocult is rich.*

I happened to know the Graeae Collective were close to MegaCorp status. Cities like the Edge where the inhabitants paid no attention to social rankings were scattered all over the globe and the Graeae were a major, wealthy presence in all of them. As far as I knew, they always had local cult leaders like these tri-rulers. There may have been an overarching head but I suspected not – the movement had a decentralised vibe.

The neural implants they developed were the best in the business. They were used for device remote control throughout the Panopticon states: on Earth, in space, and on the new planets. Most of the Graeae chose to repurpose their visual or auditory processing but many also detached some part of their peripheral nervous system and hooked their cerebral cortex directly into exoskeletons. I'd read some of them could match machine execution speeds. That tech was very useful.

Of course, their implants also worked for those with less deliberate input or output issues. The Collective paid for the production of the best tech in the solar system for disabled citizens. That's why no one in their right mind would get into a bar fight with a person in a wheelchair. Even wearing a trained suit you literally wouldn't last a minute – probably less than a second if they had the rail gun attachment and were plugged into the mains.

"A boon indeed," I repeated getting back to the problem at hand. "Someone seems to be using our games to harm our players. We think the Conundran leader might be involved. We need to identify the Warlock."

The nameless leader cackled, "But, they were not your players were they? They were outcasts in your games – people you did not care about. Why the concern for them now?"

The ruler had an excellent point. I already knew this situation was our fault.

Nemo stepped forward, "OK Mike, you're right. We were a couple of arseholes the way we implemented that looks-upgrade feature but we're doing our best to fix things."

I nodded, "We've already turned the function off and we're tracking down all the affected people. So, do you know who the Warlock is and what'll it cost us?"

The spokesman ruler pushed back his hood and said, "Fair enough. Everyone makes mistakes." He turned towards the door, "Carol!" he shouted. "Could we get some coffee and biscuits in here? We've got negotiating to do." He turned back to us, "By the way," the cultist gestured towards the figures on his left and right, "meet Craig and Sylvie. They're big fans." The pair nodded in a friendly fashion and started unbuttoning their lips before the refreshments arrived. I winced slightly.

He turned meaningfully to Nemo, "Are you free for D&D this Saturday? Kirby's coming."

WELLNESS

Edge City, September 2054

After our meeting, Nemo and I walked back to the station. Doing a deal for the identity of the Warlock had taken a couple of hours and what the tri-rulers had wanted in return surprised us. On reflection, we knew it shouldn't have.

"I sometimes forget we're the ones with god-like powers - at least in our own Worlds," I commented as we hurried along the pavement. There was a train south we reckoned we could just make if we didn't dawdle.

"Yeah, that was a big unmet need there we hadn't spotted," Nemo mused.

It didn't even break the laws of physics, I thought, which was fortunate because my brother frowned on that. In fact, it was quite the opposite – the Graeae Collective wanted our games to better represent physics for them.

Mike, Craig and Sylvie told us the Collective had recently optimized their neural implants for our games' data interfaces. Arguably, the in-game experience for every member of the Graeae was now better than my own and I used state-of-the-art visors and haptics. The vast majority of our players couldn't even match me, never mind them.

According to the cult's latest annual wellness survey, integration with our Dystopia and Utopia games was now their most highly-rated membership perk. "Even more popular than the canteen," Craig said, shaking his head, "and our chefs make a real effort with the pastries. Before the implant upgrade, our croissants always won."

Their members loved our games but they had a complaint. They were irritated that their denizens and avatars operated at organic speeds – our prediction algorithms treated them exactly as if they were standard humans. Mike argued that was wrong – they had upgraded themselves in the analog world and our systems unfairly failed to reflect that. They felt their in-game representations should have reaction times and behavioural calculation speeds at least double that of the base human model.

The tri-rulers had an interesting point. It was clear we hadn't properly accommodated cyborgs in our VR Worlds, which was both humanist and, more importantly, foolish - cyborgs were usually wealthy.

When we finally shook hands with Mike on our deal we had agreed to review the situation and make the changes to the code that we, in good faith, considered justified. We recorded our discussion as a Panopticon contract so all players could stay informed and the Graeae Collective could appeal through the Panopticon's Court of Public Opinion if we broke our word.

As we strode back to the station, Nemo and I agreed it was a reasonable request. The only downside was it would cost us more to power their denizens if they effectively got twice the cpu cycles of everyone else. The upside was once we'd upgraded their speed I reckoned we could get the Collective to spend more of their cash on us. Perhaps I could persuade them to become sponsors. With double the processing, the Graeae cult would become a major power in our game worlds. That would make our Dystopias a great channel for them to attract new members. I'd give their marketing team a call.

Once we'd got the pro quo settled, they handed over the quid. From the train that morning, Nemo had sent the Collective all the data we had on our greasy barman and the other missing folk. He'd included the grainy photograph of the man we thought was the Warlock.

The tri-rulers agreed all of the missing people had had their debts settled before they disappeared. "Follow the money," said Mike.

The individual debts were never huge but unpaid bills were frowned upon in the Panopticon nations. For our losers, it had been a major factor in their low status. The problem was usually that the lower your social scores fell, the less you could earn and the harder it got to pay the arrears - it was a vicious circle. I thought about my previous encounter with the greasy barman in Utopia Five. Perhaps I should have sympathised with him slightly more? At the time I just reckoned he was a jerk. Let's face it though, he probably was.

With some digging around, the Graeae Collective's fraud investigation department had tracked down who'd paid off the debts.

"All of them," Mike said, "were settled in WorldGov Sols by the Council of Conundra."

After that, the money trail had left the Panopticon nations and the Collective hadn't been able to follow it further. Nemo and I had looked at one another. This new information confirmed our suspicions but hadn't told us anything new.

"Did the photo of the Warlock turn up anything?" I asked.

Mike nodded. "It was tricky with that hair disguise but we finally matched it. The guy in the photo was a pre-Summer actor by the name of Walter West. He last performed in public in 2035 and hasn't been seen since."

An actor! I thought. *Where on earth did he get the money to build Conundra?*

"So, that was the last anyone ever heard of Walter West?"

"Oh no," the tri-ruler replied. "We found this." He handed me a photocopy of a cutting from the London Times. It appeared to be from a page of obituaries. "According to this," Mike said, "Walter West died in 2049."

LONDON

Edge City, September
2054

When we got to the station, Nemo said, "Give me a minute, will you? I'm desperate," and nipped into the toilets.

I felt grateful I didn't have to worry about that anymore - I'd missed my stillsuit in Conundra.

The head-up display on the inside of my goggles told me there was a train to Conundra in fifteen minutes and one to London in twenty.

Nemo returned, straightening his Inverness cape.

"I can't believe you're still wearing that," I commented, "it's 42.7 degrees."

"It hides my multitude of sins," he said, opening it up. Sewn inside his cape was an array of tiny drones. "Twelve dozen self-guided explosives, synced to new contact lenses," he looked smug. "I picked them all up from Mike. He reminded me they're strictly illegal in Conundra, but I thought it was worth the risk given we might have to fight off the local government to get your greasy barman back. I didn't see a single metal detector or weapons check the whole time I was there, so I reckon we'll get away with it. Anyway, these are mostly plastic - hard to spot."

I'd also observed the lack of security in Conundra, which was why I'd taken the risk of just throwing a long coat over my new suit. I'd started to suspect Wade Scarlet was telling the truth - Conundra didn't have the money to man their observation systems anymore and they didn't have automated monitoring like Deus or Control. The LARP state seemed extremely low-tech compared to the Panopticon.

If I was wrong, my suit would be easy for any decent security system to identify - it contained rather a lot of metal. Even my goggles could recognise a hidden exoskeleton based on gait analysis and figure density observations. On the other hand, a suit wasn't a weapon or, at least, it wasn't only a weapon. I could argue it was safety equipment. Smuggling a suit into Conundra was more likely to result in a wrist slapping than a prison sentence. I wondered if they even had prisons. My guess was they exiled their criminals to the Panopticon states. *Much cheaper*, I thought.

"I spoke to Laura just now," my brother updated me, "the Panopticon will do what they can to help us but they don't have an army. She said we'd have to make do with Ray and Catterwade."

I grimaced, "And state police are great at lost passwords, less good at international incidents."

Nemo nodded, "I considered contacting WorldGov but their troops can be a bit heavy-handed and we don't know for certain that our missing people didn't just move to Conundra with a sign-up bonus." He sighed, "If there was shared record keeping between the Panopticon states and Conundra this would have been a hell of a lot easier."

"At least the niece isn't far away. I'll go and talk to her in person - see what I can find out." Walter

West's obituary had mentioned a niece in London by name and we'd tracked her down to an address in Soho.

Nemo and I agreed that after I'd spoken to her we'd meet back in Conundra that evening.

An alert flashed up on my lens. "You'd better leg it to catch your train." I told Nemo.

"Oh," he replied carelessly, "you go find the woman and I'll see you at dinner. I need to check on something else while I'm here."

"Not your bloody security pigs?" I said, scornfully.

"I'd like to visit them before I go into battle. They're comforting."

"Why don't you just wear a fricking suit for Deus sake?" I said, shaking my head. "OK, I'll catch my train and see you at the hotel when I get back."

I left my brother happily skipping off to see his animals. One of the other services of the Graeae was their porcine organ and full body repository – in other words, the piggy bank. The basic idea was replacement organs on demand. The donors were genetically tailored to each buyer to minimize rejection. If you met with a severe enough accident, the Graeae could also circify you – transfer your head onto the body of a waiting pig.

I guessed it was a good life for the pigs: they were painstakingly cared-for, in perfect health, and the likelihood of one actually meeting its planned fate was at least a thousand to one. As an emergency backup plan though, it didn't appeal to me. Once your head was sewn on the animal, the likelihood of you ever being transferred to a primate donor body was low – there weren't many on the market and the transplant risks were high to a body that hadn't been bred with you in mind. Arguably, a clone would have been better, but WorldGov assigned them full rights as soon as the first baby was born in 2044. Anyway, humans take way too long to grow.

On the positive side, the neural implants of the Graeae could give you a fairly decent life of the mind even as a farmyard animal. Nemo reckoned it was better than being dead and I could see his point. Still, call me a luddite but I really hoped my brother never ended up running around with his head on a pig. For a start, Christmas would be a catering nightmare.

◆ ◆ ◆

The London train was already waiting at the platform when I got there. I climbed on board and settled myself into a seat. The carriage was nearly empty again, which suited me well.

The Graeae Collective had been able to find an address for Walter West's closest living relative, a niece called Amber Harris, in Soho Square. I checked with Deus who informed me she was a waitress at a cafe near her flat and was there today. I asked the chatbot to leave her a request for a conversation and five minutes later I got a message to say she'd be available at work all afternoon. *Great,* I thought. In the meantime, it would take about 90 minutes to reach London, which would give me opportunity to get familiar with my new exoskeleton.

First, I decided to practice pairing my suit with the matching observation drones. I opened the box Pam had given me. Inside, I saw half a dozen glowing red LEDs. "Go!" I commanded. If I'd wanted to be more subtle, I could have merely looked at the initiate command that had appeared on the right hand lens of my goggles.

The quadcopters rose in tandem and hovered in a two dimensional hexagon pattern parallel to the ground and just above my head. *A halo!* I thought. *Kirby would approve.*

"Observe!" the drones scattered throughout the carriage and six small displays filled my left lens. The devices apparently had full 360 cameras because each display rotated like a carousel in two spin orientations. I remembered, back in my teens, how many times I'd thrown up while I was getting my brain used to direct drone input – it was not the best week of my life.

Even now, I could barely look at the feeds without falling over. They were only of limited value to me – I'd have to turn them off or switch to a static view before I ate my lunch or I'd go full Exorcist on this train carriage and that would be somewhat anti-social. *No*, I thought, unless you had the neural implants and brain retraining the Graeae Collective provided, 360 drone feeds weren't of much use to you. They were never intended for unenhanced organics. The win was when you paired them to a combat-trained exoskeleton in autonomic mode.

That reminded me. The train had started moving and I glanced up and down the carriage. It was quiet, which was why I'd picked it. My next task was to bond the suit with me. I'd been wearing it for a few hours, so it already had some idea of how my arms and legs moved but all I had done was walk around. That was fairly limited.

I got up from my seat, stood in the aisle, stretched my arms above my head and went through the callisthenic initialisation routine. It took about twenty minutes. The idea was for the autonomic system to learn where, how far and how fast it could position my limbs if it took over, which it would do on demand or in extremis.

Everyone knew if you ran into an emergency while wearing unbonded safety equipment, it could end up pulling your arms off. *That might be better than being dead*, I thought, *but it wouldn't be a laugh a minute.* Actually, suits didn't pull limbs off all that often but mine had dislocated my shoulder a couple of times. Fortunately, my suit could usually reset that.

Eventually, I got a green light from the exoskeleton on our autonomic bond and I sat back down. I still had an hour to go until London. I stared out of the window at the passing grass fields and pondered the Graeae. I'd never had a neural implant installed but I'd thought about it more than once. My rationale for not doing so was I got a lot of the same benefits by wearing a top-end suit. Most of the processing that would be done in an implant could be done by my exoskeleton. My suit could take video and audio feeds, run local processing on them and physically control my limbs in response - or more accurately, the exoskeleton could move itself and drag my arms and legs along for the ride. Having my own nervous system in the loop would only slow things down.

What my suit couldn't do was affect my internal state: my heart, lungs, or hormone levels. It also couldn't rewire my brain. I wasn't sure I wanted it to do those things but I wondered if I might be depriving myself.

The human brain is highly interconnected and grows new neurons and synapses all the time. If I had direct data feeds into my cerebral cortex who knew what my brain might end up doing with them. It could be incredibly cool or, of course, it might drive me crazy. The suit was more predictable, which had its pros and cons. The ultimate downside to a suit was that when I took it off I lost all my enhanced function. The solution to that was obvious: don't take it off.

THE NIECE

London, September 2054

Two hours later, I was walking through the centre of London's Soho district looking for the Buttercup Cafe. That was where Deus told me I'd find Amber Harris.

The streets were heaving with bicycles pulling rickshaws or small trailers that were mostly filled with food but occasionally furniture or bric-a-brac. I managed to dodge my way across the street to a small, cheerful tea shop with tables and chairs on the pavement outside. An elderly couple were sitting in the sunshine. Otherwise, the place was empty.

The door of the cafe was propped open and I walked into a relatively cool interior. A friendly-looking woman with greying blond hair and an apron was clearing one of the tables.

"Hi, Amber?"

"Lee?" she asked in response. "Please sit down. Shall I make us something to drink?"

◆ ◆ ◆

We sat at a table outside and Amber poured tea into two bright yellow mugs. She told me she'd need to keep an eye on her customers while we talked. As far as I could tell, that was just the aged pair who were one table over.

"So you want to know about Uncle Walt?" she asked.

"Then Walter really was his name?"

"Yes," Amber replied. "Walter Harris. He changed it to West years ago. It was his stage name you know?"

I asked her to tell me what she remembered of her uncle.

"He was my Dad's brother and we used to see a lot of him before the Hot Summer. He was a repertory actor, which seemed to mean he'd go away for a few months to work then be back for a while living with us and doing odd jobs for Dad's plumbing business." She paused in consideration, "He wasn't a bad plumber."

"But he stopped visiting after '36?"

"Yes. At first we had thought we'd see a lot more of him because his theatre had burned down, but he told us he'd got a new gig – something long term. He did that for well over ten years. We didn't see much of him. They kept him busy, apparently."

I had a sudden thought, "Where had he been in rep before '36?"

"He mostly worked the south coast," she replied, "but right before the Summer he joined a group in Colchester. I don't think he'd even gone on stage there before the whole place was burned to the ground – the entire city! Of course, it's called Conundra now since they rebuilt," she sipped her tea. "That's where he got his new job – in some kind of long-running role. We guessed that made sense because they'd need a lot of actors there. Not that I ever saw his play, I've never been to Conundra. I'm not sure it's my cup of tea." She jiggled her mug cheerfully.

"He didn't come into any money? A legacy or anything?"

"Uncle Walt?" she said scornfully. "He never had two Sols to rub together."

This was making less and less sense to me. "Did you ever meet any of his work colleagues?" I asked.

"Colleagues?" she repeated thoughtfully. "There were a few at his wake. Two men of about Uncle Walt's age who looked just like him! It was quite uncanny at his funeral. Walter West had always been famous for his hair, you know? He looked like Albert Einstein but with extra big eyebrows. The two colleagues did too. They must have played a lot of mad professors." She laughed, "The men said they were Uncle Walt's understudies so he must have been important - a lead! With two understudies! And we never even knew." Amber sounded like she had been posthumously impressed.

"Was that everyone?" I asked, "There was no glamorous woman at the funeral?"

Amber shook her head. "No, I'd definitely remember that. I don't think there was anyone else." She paused, "But we could check the video feeds?"

Amber pulled her phone out of her bag and brought up the drone feeds from the funeral of Walter Harris-West, "We wanted to commemorate him with his family name and his stage name," she explained. "It seemed right somehow. I used his stage name for the obituary."

That would explain why even the Graeae hadn't found any drone footage of the wake. Since it was just a group of people standing around chatting it wasn't that easy for Deus or Control to locate a funeral without a name to search on.

We watched a static view from a single drone that must have been hovering above. It swept occasionally across the small group, who were standing in a park somewhere.

"Oh, there he is," said Amber pointing, "I remember now. That nice man wearing glasses. I think he was the theatre accountant or something. Very quiet. I'd completely forgotten about him."

I peered at a slight figure at the back of the group, who was wearing a modest, tweed suit and a slightly old fashioned hat.

It was Alex Lidenbrock.

COMRADES

Conundra, September 2054

At just after 9 p.m. I walked into the main bar in the Fogg Hotel and ordered a milkshake. I felt I'd earned it.

I looked around for my brother. Nemo was sitting at a table in the private bar with a grizzled man in his fifties who was wearing a suit and fedora. Next to him was a thin woman in a trench coat which, despite the heat, was buttoned up and tied at the waist. From her apparent size and mass, my goggles informed me, she was concealing a heavyweight exoskeleton.

I felt a wave of relief at seeing my old comrades. When it came down to it, Nemo and I were just a couple of computer programmers. Ray and Catterwade actually knew how to handle themselves.

I hadn't seen either of them in several months. While Laura had been stationed at Angelsea, Ray and Catterwade had been away on some hush-hush mission. I didn't know anything about it and they weren't allowed to discuss the subject. Nemo and I hadn't been able to locate them through the Panopticon.

I was sure Ray found the secrecy frustrating but Catterwade hardly spoke anyway - this just gave her one more thing to be reticent about. I knew that Catterwade's partner Stone and their kids were still roaming the country with their horse and cart, fixing downed power lines and drones for the Panopticon. I expected Catterwade would join them now she was back.

I sat down and smiled at the trio. Nemo and Ray grinned back. Even Catterwade managed to look marginally less gloomy - for a brief moment.

"Your brother has been bringing us up to date," said Ray. "What's the news from London?"

I glanced at Nemo.

"Don't worry," he said, "I've already jammed the microphones – just in case we're wrong and someone is listening."

Now that I knew for certain we were unobserved, I filled them in on my interview with Amber Harris.

"Interesting," said Ray, straightening his tie, "so, your new friend Alex may know more than he's letting on."

"Yeah," I replied. "I'll confront him tomorrow - I'm not getting anything from the net."

On my journey back from London, I'd tried to find out everything I could about the so-called Professor Alex Lidenbrock. Unfortunately, that was almost nothing. Lidenbrock was obviously an assumed name, so that didn't get me anywhere. His image didn't turn up any additional data on a Deus or Control search either.

Alex looked like he was in his thirties, so I guessed he could have been twentyish when Conundra was founded. If he'd been in the city ever since then, the Panopticon would have almost no information on him. People changed a lot from when they were young and photos of him then wouldn't necessarily be matched with him now. Nemo and I both knew it was easy to disappear in your teens.

I had located Alex in our Control world sim at the now-known 4D coordinates of Walter West's funeral. I entered the sim with a zero-opacity avatar and followed him back and forward in time. He and the two Warlock lookalikes had taken a train from Conundra to London together, gone straight to the wake and returned by the same route later in the day. They had disappeared from Control the moment the train crossed the Conundra city limits.

Unfortunately, what I'd seen in the sim told me nothing. I'd listened in on their conversations, but they were innocuous, even banal. Small talk as if they barely knew one another. For most of the journey back, Alex read a newspaper and the two actors talked about hair products. The funeral service clearly hadn't inspired more existential discussions.

I had just finished telling the others about the dead-end I'd hit on Professor Alex Lidenbrock when, suddenly, the doors to the bar swung open to reveal a tall figure in a homburg hat. The silhouette paused for a moment, framed in the opening.

I was reminded that everyone around here knew their stagecraft.

SPADEWORK

*Conundra, September
2054*

"Ray and Catterwade," I said, "meet Pip Marlowe, Private Eye and secret agent of the Panopticon."

Marlowe, who had strode in and sat down at our table, looked aghast.

"The microphones are disabled," said Nemo apologetically. "We aren't really so indiscreet. Lee and I are pretty sure these two are secret agents for the Panopticon too, if we're being honest here." He pointed at our newly arrived friends.

Now it was Ray and Catterwade's turn to look aghast. My brother, on the other hand, looked smug. He believed that if the Panopticon forced everyone else to reveal the truth about themselves, they shouldn't be allowed to hide stuff either. He had a point.

Pip shrugged, "Useful day?"

I nodded, "We've picked up a few leads. We confirmed the Conundran Council is connected with the disappearances – they paid off the debts of the missing people. We just don't know how far the involvement extends or what's happening to the folk who disappear. We also know the Warlock isn't who he appears to be – and there seem to have been at least three of them."

Pip Marlowe's expression turned grim, "I haven't been slack either," she said, and slapped a photograph down on the table in front of us. It was of a smiling young woman with a mass of wavy brown hair. The image looked like a mugshot from an HR file and it was clearly the person who had been shot in front of me two days earlier – just ten minutes after I'd arrived in Conundra.

"Her name was Katy Potts. She moved to Conundra two years ago and got a job at the Department of Mystery and Intrigue. I talked to her colleagues, who told me she hadn't shown up at the office for two days. They were worried about her – she had a reputation for conscientiousness.

She hadn't been seen at her rooms either, so I phoned London. The Panopticon still had an official image for her on file." Pip looked at me, "Is this the woman you saw?"

I nodded.

"What did she work on?" asked Ray.

"HR for Domestic Services."

Ray looked blank.

"Managing hotel workers, cleaners, cooks, waiters – that kind of thing. Making sure they get assigned where they're needed and checking their work and their acting," said Pip. "Domestics are meant to be almost invisible to guests but they're fundamental to the operation of the stories here."

"People like bartenders." I said, thoughtfully.

"Yeah. According to a friend of Katy's at the council, she'd been worried recently about how many new arrivals had suddenly walked out on their jobs and apparently gone back to the Panopticon." Pip shrugged, "These things happen – some folk don't like it here – but Katy Potts had been trying to work out why they left and whether the Council could have managed them better to keep them. She'd been attempting to track the recent leavers down in the Panopticon nations to interview them – she still had plenty of friends there to look things up for her. She was worried because she couldn't locate most of them."

Ray, Nemo and I looked at one another. It sounded like Katy Potts was investigating the same problem we were – only from the other side.

"That reminds me," continued Pip, "I also showed the photograph of your greasy barman around."

We leaned forward.

"I found him or, at least, I found the hostel he's staying at. I didn't catch him there in person."

I cursed.

"I did speak to the manager. The barman had told him he'd be starting work tonight at that dive you visited yesterday." The P.I. looked at me, "The Leviathan Bar."

"We need to go and get him right now!" I exclaimed.

"Might be easier said than done," she replied, "I went there and spoke to that shifty woman who runs the place. They have a private function on tonight and the security seems incredibly tight. The show kicks off at midnight. Your barman isn't due on shift until then." The P.I. grimaced, "The weird thing is, I can't find out anything official about the function and the woman owner didn't seem to know much either - or at least she wasn't admitting anything. I talked to my contacts at the Council and there's nothing on record about a party there. It doesn't sound like it's part of any of the standard storylines."

Pip looked around at us all. It felt to me like we needed to grab the barman as quickly as possible before anything happened to him. At the very least, we needed to keep him under observation. I wondered what tools we had.

"Catterwade," I said, "I know recording devices are contraband in Conundra, but since drones are your specialty I'm guessing you brought some anyway?"

She silently lifted a small attaché case onto the table and opened it.

"Stealth badges," said Ray. "Take one. It'll grab on to you and record. Tap it once to turn it on. Tap it twice and it'll take off and hover – film you from above. Everyone apply one please. They're high power. That means they'll only last an hour so be sparing - wait for the action."

I picked up a metal badge and pressed it against my suit.

Next, Catterwade pulled a large drone out of a bag.

"A PPD - Portable Panopticon Device," Ray continued. "It ascends to 3,000 feet where it's almost invisible. It'll take end-to-end encrypted feeds from our stealthies here," he pointed at my badge, "and rebroadcast them to the nearest official Panopticon relay, which we've positioned at 10,000 feet above our heads. That's just inside WorldGov airspace so Panopticon drones and UAVs are officially allowed to fly there. Before you ask, the high power signals from your badges should punch through the city's jamming to the PPD. Everything we do here will be in full view of the whole Panopticon supernation from the moment we turn the stealthies on."

He paused and looked around at us all, "That's in breach of every treaty between the Panopticon and WorldGov. We only enable broadcast if we believe an innocent Panopticon citizen is in danger. In this case, Lee, that'll be your greasy barman. We four don't count as innocent by the way – we chose to take our chances here."

"What about firepower?" I asked.

Catterwade opened her backpack and we all peered inside.

"One phalanx of fully programmable attack drones. Kill decision-enabled." Ray grinned evilly, "They'll take out anyone armed – apart from us, of course." He glanced at Pip, "We'll add you too."

"And you brought this all in yourselves?" Nemo whistled, "Conundra's Head of Security really needs to go on a training course."

I had just asked Pip to go back and watch the Leviathan in case our barman arrived early, when the door to the bar swung open again and a man stuck his head inside.

"Lee! Thank goodness I've found you!" exclaimed Professor Alex Lidenbrock.

THE PROF

Conundra, September 2054

Catterwade nonchalantly closed her attaché case and backpack, and slipped the PPD back into her bag, while Alex dashed over to me looking relieved and distracted. He suddenly stopped when he noticed my companions.

"Professor Alex Lidenbrock," I said pointedly, "Meet my friends."

"I've been looking for you all day!" he exclaimed. "I asked Phyllida to let me know when you got back to the hotel."

"Here I am," I said. "What's up?"

He looked slightly taken aback by my cold tone. I was well aware Alex knew more about what was going on in this city than he'd let on.

"Err," he started, "I looked into your Leviathan story today. I thought you were probably exaggerating about a bullet hitting only a foot away from you, but you seemed sensible so I wanted to double check – what you'd described would be way outside our safety rules for guests. I went to the alley you mentioned and found a bullet hole. An actual bullet hole! None of our actors should be firing live ammunition. We only shoot blanks."

He looked flustered and gazed at my new intimidating friends, "I checked what Concordia Clarke had told you about trialing a new story, but I couldn't find any details about it on the systems." He swallowed, "I tried calling Concordia but she fobbed me off. This is most irregular. I came to see if you'd found out anything more?"

"Did you talk to the Warlock?" I asked, curious about his reaction.

He looked uncomfortable, "Err... no. It's not really his area of expertise."

"Why were you worried?" I pressed.

"Well," he blinked, "I wouldn't want anyone to get hurt. We can't have an actor firing real bullets! Someone might get killed for goodness sake!"

Again my gut told me, despite everything, to trust Professor Lidenbrock. I glanced at Ray, who nodded.

I was about to tell Alex about why we were all really here in Conundra when the bar doors swung open again. Phyllida Fogg stepped in and said, "Lee, there's a phone call for you. He's a rather strange-sounding man." She paused, "He says his name is Mike?"

MIKE

Conundra, September
2054

We left a confused-looking Alex sitting at the table under the cool eyes of Catterwade and took Mike's call in one of the booths in the main lobby. Nemo and Ray insisted on squashing themselves into the box with me. Ray only just managed to get the door closed. I wished the bloody Victorians had invented conference phones.

"Lee Sands?" I heard the unmistakably sinister voice of the tri-ruler of the local technocult.

"Hey Mike, have you found anything?" I asked, pushing Nemo's elbow out of my armpit.

"Yes," he hissed, "I bumped into your brother at the pig sanctuary this afternoon. He asked me to check into something else for you." I looked at Nemo, who nodded. "The Graeae Collective has some influence on the greynet. Nemo wanted us to listen for any chatter about Conundra. Something did come to our attention. There are rumours the city is offering some new...." Mike paused, "specialist experiences. Things you can no longer do under the all-seeing-eye of the Panopticon."

I thought about Concordia Clarke mentioning new products. "I heard." I said. "Sex and drugs?"

Was that what they were hiding? I wondered. Drug-fueled orgies weren't illegal under WorldGov, just disapproved of by the average Panopticon citizen. Potentially embarrassing, but hardly worth a deadly cover up. You could just go to Edge City to do that kind of thing anyway if you could live with the social hit.

"We suspect something more... permanent," Mike breathed.

"Tattooing?" I asked.

"We believe you had better do some digging from there," said Mike, ignoring me. "We have acquired the contact number for tourists interested in these services: Conundra 666." He rang off, leaving us all still crammed into the phone box.

"OK," I said. "Let's give this a try. Be quiet."

As I dialed 666, it occurred to me that automatic telephone switches were definitely not a Victorian invention. Maybe they'd installed them in the Nostalgia section. The phone connected.

"Can I help you?" came an electronically-disguised voice. It didn't sound familiar but it would have been a crap disguise if it had.

I decided this would be more plausible if I played myself. "This is Lee Sands. I'm in Conundra and I've been recommended your specialist services."

There was a pause on the other end of the line. "Do you have the password?"

Here goes nothing, I thought. "Leviathan," I replied.

♦ ♦ ♦

The voice on the other end was silent for a moment. "That will do nicely. We're glad you've contacted us. May I ask what you're interested in?"

"I heard about the new Conundra experience packages on the greynet before I arrived. I'd like to get something scheduled in this week while I'm here. I'm prepared to pay extremely well for your... discretion. Name your price."

I could practically hear lips being licked. "Are you interested in male or female?"

"Male," I said, thinking of our greasy barman.

"Ah, we do have one of those but he's already booked in for tonight. Would you like to come along and observe? We'll try to organise you a lead role later in the week."

"Where do I need to be?"

"The Leviathan Bar in the Gothic Zone," the voice replied, "At midnight."

"Is there a dress code? Do I need to bring anything?" I asked, desperately trying to get more information about the service the voice was describing - although I already had a skin-crawling suspicion.

"Don't worry, we'll provide the... equipment. Wear something you don't mind getting rather messy," the artificial voice gave a friendly chuckle. "We all know the blood never washes out."

Feeling sick, I put the phone down. Ray opened the door and we spilled out into the lobby.

"Well, I guess we know what Concordia Clarke's new premium product range is," said Ray.

I nodded, "Sounds like snuff minibreaks."

SHOWTIME

Conundra, September 2054

W e dashed back into the private bar and updated the others on our new information.

Alex looked stunned and confused, "Snuff minibreaks?" he muttered in disbelief.

I realised we'd have to fill him in as we went along. He was miles behind on the exposition. Not that it mattered - as a museum curator he couldn't really help us with this fight.

"It looks to us like our greasy barman is about to get executed," I told them.

"Showtime," agreed Nemo.

We all thought about the private function at the Leviathan bar where our bartender would be making his debut and likely exit tonight.

"The Leviathan event starts at midnight and it's ten o'clock now," said Catterwade, looking at her watch. "The security is likely to be heavy. Let's assume they'll have at least a team of goons, plus there'll be non-combatants. The victim will be present, of course, and we'll need to get him out of there alive." She frowned, "We can't just go in guns blazing."

"And we know their heavies are armed because they shot Katy Potts," I added, wondering how the Council had kept their thugs under wraps.

Ray and Catterwade looked at their stash of weaponry. "This might be enough," said Catterwade, "but I'd prefer more boots on the ground. We only have two or three fighters?" She looked at Pip, who shook her head, "Two. That's if we include Lee's suit," She grimaced, "and we know the suits have limitations."

"What we really need," Ray pointed out glumly, "is a human army. But it's not like there's a legion of Panopticonners sitting round here waiting for a fight that we could dragoon."

I had a thought, "Hold my milkshake."

THE ROMAN

*Between Conundra
and Edge City,
September 2054 -
Earlier that day*

Sitting on the train that morning, I'd told Nemo about Boudicca and her part in the history of Conundra.

"So what happened after she burned the city down?" he asked.

"Then things get more hazy," I told him. "Two threads of events appear to have kicked off."

I emptied out a bowl of sugar cubes onto the table.

"Firstly, the Romans woke up. Boudicca had only managed to sack Camulodunum because most of the Roman army in Britain were in Wales. Here," I placed a handful of cubes at the top left of the table, which I'd decided represented Roman Britain.

"How many?"

"Ten thousand highly-trained, kick-ass troops. Plus the military governor Suetonius Paulinus. They were all on Angelsea."

"Kirby's place," Nemo said thoughtfully.

"Yeah. The Romans were slaughtering druids – they were the learned class of Britons back then and used to hang out there."

"Like Kirby!"

"Indeed," I nodded. "When Boudicca's army razed Camulodunum," I put another pile of cubes on the right hand side of the table, about half way down, "the Roman army heard about it and started marching south. At the same time, the Celts started south themselves to burn the city of

Londinium next." I put a single cube a little bit down from Conundra.

"And Londinium was pretty close to the Celts."

"The Celtic army was less than a hundred miles from their next target. The Roman army was 300 miles away with a water-crossing in between. *And* the Romans didn't definitely know Londinium was where Boudicca was headed." I could see Nemo was listening raptly - he loved a military story. "Now, Romans only march maybe 15 miles a day if they're heading for a battle. It was going to take them ages to get to Londinium. By then, the place would be a smouldering heap. So Governor Suetonius and a couple of his men jumped on horses and galloped ahead. With ride changes they could do 30 miles a day."

"Unless Suetonius and his mates were a Roman version of the 'A Team' I don't see how that helps. Was he going to fight the whole Celtic army?"

"It gave Suetonius better information than he currently had, I guess." I paused, "Do you want a sandwich or anything from the buffet?"

"No!" he replied. "I'm enjoying the story - get on with it."

"The Celts must have been dawdling or bickering or something because Suetonius and his centurion gang got to Londinium before them. The local population begged him to stay and help them against Boudicca, who was definitely on route, but Suetonius made the call that Londinium was unsaveable and rode back to his own army." I paused, "He left the unlucky Londoners to their fate."

"Which was presumably to be burned to death by the rampaging Boudicca and her army of crazy Celts," stated Nemo. "Sensible move by Suetonius. The city was clearly doomed. And I think it was unlucky Londiniumers."

"Londiniumions?" I hazarded, "The upshot was, by the time they'd finished off Londinium, the Celts had a triumphant army of 100,000 vs the Roman 10,000."

"10 to 1?" Nemo sucked his teeth.

"But the Romans understood their advantages. Their soldiers were trained killing machines. The Celts were mostly wagon loads of farmers, kids, and grannies armed with pitchforks."

"Did they have pitchforks then?"

"It was the Iron Age, so presumably."

"I thought a Roman invasion marked the end of an Iron Age?"

"That was only twenty years earlier. I'd guess the Celts were still Iron Age and the Romans weren't. Like a wise man said, the future had arrived in Britain - it just wasn't evenly distributed yet. Anyway, let me get on with my story," I glared at the interruption.

I continued, "Historians reckon Suetonius got back to his legions and had them set up on ground he chose. He put most of his men in a narrow valley with hills on either side and a wood behind. He knew he had to lure the huge Celtic army into a funnel with what seemed to be a tiny group of Romans at the end of it. The Celts took the bait. In reality, that tiny group was a meat grinder."

"The Celts broke?"

"Yes, but they were trapped by their own troops, carts, and followers behind. And by the landscape, of course. The Romans slaughtered everyone. That was probably unsurprising – it was, after all, their hobby."

"Blimey," said Nemo. "This was 2,000 years ago? All that destruction was about trying to take back control of Britain from Rome?"

"Actually," I shrugged, "it wasn't really. The Celtic leaders had been perfectly happy collaborating until their loans got called in. The rebellion was about debt. If Roman moneylenders like Seneca hadn't foreclosed, suddenly making a load of key folk in Britain destitute, then the revolt would never have happened. 200,000 people were killed by dodgy lending practices."

"What about Boudicca?"

"Some historians reckon she killed herself to avoid capture but no one really knows what happened to her."

"Hmm. I guess it's safe to assume she's dead?"

CONN

Conundra, September
2054

Handing my drink to Ray, I dashed off in search of Phyllida Fogg. I found her behind the main bar, polishing glasses.

"What's the quickest way to get to the Celtic camp?"

"I guess you could borrow my motorcycle?" she replied.

I sprinted back into the private bar and informed the others I was off to find us some heavies of our own and I'd meet them in front of the Leviathan for the assault. "Assume I'll have at least ten men with me, probably armed with axes."

Alex piped up that he could get floor plans for the building, "If that would help?"

Ray agreed gratefully.

While Ray and Alex were discussing that, I took Catterwade aside for a quick chat. She nodded her understanding. Finally, I left them all to it. They'd do a far better job on the military planning than I would.

I dug out my paper city map and stared at it through my new goggles, then I enabled WorldGov's GPS - I didn't need to be in the Panopticon to pick that up.

As I dashed back through the main bar, Phyllida indicated her motorbike was in the backyard.

"Thanks!" I yelled. "By the way, did the Celts hold their Royal Challenge today?"

"Oh! Yes," she smiled. "Thanks very much for telling me about that. Paul and Esther enjoyed the competition a great deal. One of those splendid boys from the WorldGov irrigation projects won, I believe."

Well done Dave! I thought, and then mentally winced. *I hope you're not too drunk by now.*

I ran out to the yard. There was a bike there resting on its stand with a helmet hanging off the seat. I grabbed that and strapped it on, flicking the visor up so I could use my own goggles. On my own head-up display, I queried the fastest route to the Celtic camp. It was about two miles west. My goggles calculated I could be there in ten minutes. I reckoned it would then take at least half an hour to get people back from the camp to the Leviathan on foot. That meant when I reached the Celts I'd have less than 30 minutes to convince a group of people I barely knew to join me in a potentially deadly battle to save someone they'd never met. *It might be tight*, I thought.

I kicked the motorbike into life and rolled out onto the street outside the hotel. In AR mode, my right lens highlighted the route I needed to take. Before I started, I dug a box out of my pocket and opened it up. Inside were the quadcopters I'd paired with my suit that afternoon. On my verbal command, the six drones flew out and assumed their baseline halo configuration just above my head and out of my eye line. These drones weren't connected to the Panopticon like Catterwade's, and they weren't armed, but they would give the autonomic functions of my suit a hell of a lot of real-time situational information to work with. In my opinion, that was better than guns.

Damn! I hadn't thought to check if my new exoskeleton was motorcycle-trained – I hadn't specifically requested that from Pam. I looked at the bike through my goggles and issued a query to my suit. The response flashed up as a set of specifications and a message in red that rolled across the AR display: "VEHICLE SUPPORTED". *Thank Deus for that*, I thought, *and thank Pam, of course, she always went above and beyond.*

I could ride a motorbike but I wasn't well-practised and I didn't have time to brush up my skills. "You have the conn." I said aloud to my suit.

It knew where we were going.

ARMY

Conundra, September 2054

Five minutes later, the bike screeched to a halt about a quarter of a mile beyond the western edge of the city, in what looked like a muddy tent village. At least, it looked like a tent village once I'd opened my eyes. The new suit's driving was going to take some getting used to.

"You have arrived at your destination," announced my goggles. The suit had clearly noticed I wasn't in a position to observe the head-up display. "You now have the conn."

"Bloody hell! You can ride," came a voice.

I looked around to see a guy in a Viking helmet holding what looked like a horn of ale and sitting on a low tree stump. I grinned and didn't correct him on who was doing the driving, "I'm looking for the Royal Champion?"

"Dave? In the main arena. He's tossing," he replied.

I hoped that was cabers not his lunch – or anything else for that matter – or my best laid plans were going to go very awry. I needed Dave and his mates somewhat sober.

From what I'd heard, I reckoned the Celts were on holiday from the Panopticon to crack heads away from their disapproving grannies. *Let's see if they'll crack any for me*, I thought. The Viking had pointed towards the middle of the tented area and I hurried in that direction.

◆ ◆ ◆

The main arena turned out to be a tramped area of grass about the size of a tennis court. Canvas tents were pitched around the outside, facing in, and most of them were full of young people drinking beer. Standing in the centre of it all was Dave the Celt: bare-chested, and surrounded by adoring fans and carelessly thrown tree trunks.

He turned, caught sight of me, and strode over, grinning broadly. The new Royal Champion was wearing a huge, golden belt and very little else. I reckoned he looked like a cross between Wonder Woman and a man wearing a freshly spray-painted male corset that had been bought in a hurry from a Victorian outfitter. I decided not to mention that.

"Lee! Your idea worked! Look what I've got," he pointed with both thumbs at his new metallic girdle. "It appeared about five minutes after the tournament finished. A woman cycled in and rushed up with it. The paint was still wet." He laughed, "We're calling it the accessory after the fact."

I snorted, "I knew you'd win. What did you challenge on? Cart-pulling? Caber-tossing? Hole-digging?"

"We had an ironmongery-themed punning competition," he replied, smirking.

That showed what I knew.

"What did you do after you won?" I asked, recognising a cue when it was called for.

"Glad you axed. We all got hammered, then I went back to my tent for a..."

"Thanks for that, I get the point."

"That's what..."

"OK!" I said. Now I was wishing I was the hit-a-punner-with-an-axe type. "I'm glad the challenge went well because I need a favour from you. Or maybe your King?" I looked at him seriously, "Someone needs rescuing."

"For real?" Dave asked.

I nodded, "For real."

◆ ◆ ◆

Ten minutes later, Dave and I were standing in the main tent talking to the Celtic King who was nodding nervously. He seemed nice enough - if a bit weedy. *This guy is no Boudicca*, I thought, and frowned.

Most of the camp had drifted in to see what was going on. I realised if I was going to round up an army, I'd have to do it myself. I grabbed a wobbly-looking wooden stool, climbed up on it and shouted to the room.

"My name is Lee Sands!"

There was a buzz of recognition. Most of the people in the tent were under thirty - this was *my* demographic.

"My friend, Dave the Champion," I paused while everyone cheered, "and I have discovered someone in Conundra has kidnapped one of my Dystopia players," much booing ensued, "and is about to murder them!"

It was a bit of an over-simplification but I didn't have time for War and Peace here.

"This is not a game," I said. "It's real and it's actually dangerous. I need help to take out the villains and get our player back," there was silence. "Genuine head-cracking will be involved." I added.

The room roared.

◆ ◆ ◆

A few minutes later, Dave and the King were organising the volunteers – it looked like the whole camp was gathering up all the axes and pitchforks they could get their hands on.

"There's something else you must do," I said, forcefully, to Dave, "I need everyone to be wearing battle woad. Every fighter *must be blue in the face.* Absolutely no exceptions!"

He grinned, "That suits us fine."

BLUE

Conundra, September
2054

At a quarter to midnight, I arrived at the Leviathan with just under a hundred blue-painted Celts.

We'd left the weedy monarch behind at the camp - the Warlock, whatever he was, was supposedly due to turn up there later that evening to congratulate the Challenge winner. The King would bring him up to speed with what we were up to.

When we arrived at the bar, Ray and Catterwade immediately started to brief the fighters on the plan of action. Catterwade intended to rely on strategy and our, hopefully, vastly superior firepower. She proposed to send her drones in first to get a view of the inside of the building and take out as many enemy combatants as possible before any humans exposed themselves. Once the place was disarmed and secure, the rest of us would run in. Catterwade and I would go first because we had the only body armour. The aim was no Panopticon casualties – we had drones and we intended to use them.

Pip Marlowe had been watching the bar for the last hour. "There are about a dozen goons in there dressed as Roman centurions," she told us. "The bad news is, they all looked like they were armed with handguns and your barman was already inside by the time I got here. There were at least two heavies on the door so I couldn't get him out quietly."

"What's the good news?" asked Nemo.

"They could have had submachine guns, and they aren't even wearing suits – they clearly weren't expecting trouble."

I nodded, that was indeed good news. I pulled on my gloves. Catterwade and I should be proof against handguns and the offensive drones would shoot anyone else carrying a weapon. Anyway, we'd let them clean the place out before we went in.

"What about the Celts?" asked my brother.

"Lee asked me to program the drones not to attack anyone blue," said Catterwade, gazing at my army of new arrivals, "I'd thought that a strange request at the time, but I can now see the logic."

I wandered over to check on Nemo. "I'm going to wait outside with Alex," he said. "Neither of us is a fighter and I've decided Peppa deserves a long and happy life."

I was relieved. I suspected it was marginally easier to manage my little brother in his current form factor.

For old times' sake, I checked my pocket watch. It was nearly midnight. I walked over to Catterwade and nodded, pulled up my hood and settled my goggles. "You have the conn." I said to my suit. It could take over from here. As I may have said before, I was a computer programmer not a vigilante.

LEVIATHAN

Conundra, September 2054

Catterwade and I – or more correctly my suit – waited until the sound of explosions and gunfire had stopped before we pushed our way in through the front door. My suit drones zipped ahead. They should give me sufficient warning to get clear of anything short of an explosion that'd take out the whole place. We were betting the Leviathan hadn't been rigged for that.

We walked slowly and carefully through the main bar, which was strewn with broken glass. I stepped over the dead body of a centurion with a magnum gripped in his hand. I momentarily wondered if it was the same guy I'd seen the day before with a choc ice.

According to the floorplans of the place, there was a large back room through a door behind the bar and another door out of that into an alley at the rear of the building. Ray had already stationed a couple of drones and a few Celts there. I could see several dozen of the offensive drones still sweeping the bar. If anyone moved with a gun they would have no chance – our backs were covered.

Catterwade signaled one of the 'copters towards the entrance to the back room. She made a fist and then opened it. The drone flew over, attached itself to the door and exploded, blowing it off its hinges. Most of the remaining drones streamed through.

I heard a yell of fear from inside the room, some gunfire and then an ominous silence - although I thought I could hear faint sobbing.

Several of my personal drones zipped through the open door and relayed back the scene. A handful of centurions were lying on the ground. Dead, I assumed. The rest were spaced around the room with their fists clenched, having thrown down their weapons. The goons had clearly realised disarming themselves would stop the drones attacking them.

Since I'd arrived, it had been blindingly obvious Conundra was in the tech Iron Age. Their subjects would have no chance in a fight against Panopticon drones. However, our machines had ethical limits – they were all hardcoded not to hurt a human unless that person was armed and threatening. An unarmed centurion had nothing to fear from *them*.

The quadcopters buzzed around, waiting for a kill criterion to be triggered but none of the men even glanced at the guns on the floor – they were clearly well-trained. *These heavies may have been disarmed but they haven't surrendered.* They still looked ready for a fight, I thought. I grinned, I was sure our Celts could provide one.

My personal drones did a 360 sweep. In the far corner, a Roman senator was kneeling on the floor, crying. Pressed against the right-hand wall I saw my greasy barman. I strode into the room and stood between him and the remaining goons.

The centurions stared warily at me. Big as they were, no one in their right mind would start a fistfight with someone in a military exoskeleton. Theoretically, I thought, I *could* take out an unarmed person in my suit. I glanced up at the recording drones above me. However, unless they attacked me first, beating a bare human to a pulp would also pulverize my social scores. The Panopticon was watching. I reckoned we needed organics to end this, not machines. That was why we'd brought a human army – for some manual downvoting.

Catterwade signaled Ray to send them in. It was time to go Boudicca on these Roman arses. The room would clearly only hold about twenty of our Celts at a time – the rest would just have to wait outside for their turn.

STEVE

*Conundra, September
2054*

Twelve blue-painted men poured into the room through the door to the front bar.

The newly arrived Celts were mostly carrying sticks and axes. They squared off facing the centurions who stood their ground.

"What the hell," said a grinning Dave. He threw down his axe and ran at the nearest Roman, wrapping his colossal arms around him and barreling him to the ground. The rest of the group whooped, chucked down their own weapons, and joined him.

Given the more-or-less unlimited number of giant Celts queuing outside to get a punch in on a Roman, and the drones overhead guaranteeing no centurion was going to pull a weapon, I wasn't concerned about the conclusion. *Those Celts are really going for it,* I thought.

Catterwade had stalked over to the sobbing senator in the corner of the room and was talking quietly to him. He'd stopped crying but started to look more terrified - if that were possible. PPD drones hovered silently above us, streaming the whole scene live for the Panopticon nations.

I turned to the greasy barman behind me, who looked dazed but otherwise unhurt. I noticed he was dressed in a steampunk outfit and his wrists were tied with plastic cuffs. I cut them off and held out my hand. "Lee Sands," I said, "pleased to meet you."

He rubbed his arms then reached to take my grip. "Steve, Steve Johnson." He whistled, "You arrived just in the nick of time. That Roman guy crying over there was *literally* about to stab me through the heart with a *solid gold dagger* while these two wankers held my arms," he kicked both of the dead bodies lying nearby. "What a bunch of arseholes." We both shook our heads at the infamy of Roman senators.

"What happened then?" I asked.

"Well," he continued enthusiastically, "about a thousand drones suddenly appeared – I mean *literally materialised* – they didn't even fly in or anything. It must be some new Panopticon tech they're keeping a secret. I always knew they had stuff like that. Anyway, then that Senator guy drops his knife and sticks up his hands yelling, 'Don't shoot! Don't shoot! Help me Mummy!' What a wimp."

Steve was waving his arms around and miming the actions as well as doing the voices. I realised he wouldn't make the ideal witness in court.

"Then the guys holding me tried to draw their weapons, which was a dumb thing to do because the drones made their heads *literally explode*. It was cool."

I looked down at the bodies, whose heads were clearly intact and who appeared to have been shot in the chest.

"Then the others got the message and stood stock still," he froze for a second to make sure I understood the concept, "like statues! Exactly where they were - didn't move a muscle, didn't touch anything. Then, less than one millisecond later, you and your friend arrived. Then all the blue weirdos appeared." He gazed at a large Celt who picked up a Roman and slammed him down on a table, which promptly collapsed. "They seem to be enjoying themselves," the barman paused in thought, "I wonder if they'll want a drink afterwards?" He looked around, "There's going to be a hell of a lot of sweeping up to do in here tomorrow."

You can take the man out of the bar, but you can't take the bar out of the man, I thought. His eyewitness account sounded about as accurate as most, I suspected. I guessed this place would be in need of a new manager now. I smiled, Steve Johnson may have just earned himself a pub - he already seemed to be practicing the origin story.

"Did you see anyone else, apart from the Romans?" I asked.

"Oh, the woman and the guy slipped out the back as soon as the action started," he replied.

WARLOCK

Conundra, September 2054

Twenty minutes later, the centurions were trussed up on the floor of the bar. Half the Celts were sitting around comparing their incipient black eyes, and Steve had roped the rest into carrying kegs of beer up from the cellar and finding unbroken glasses to serve it in.

Catterwade still had the Roman Senator in a firm grip and Ray, Nemo and the others had joined us to survey the scene.

"I can't believe I let this happen!" muttered Alex, dragging his hand through his hair.

The front door was hanging off its hinges. One of the Celts had managed to find a screwdriver somewhere and was attempting to rehang it, when Dave strode through. In one hand, he was holding a bitterly complaining Concordia Clarke. In the other, was a silent Wade Scarlet - Clarke's previously cheerful second-in-command.

"Take your hands off me!" demanded Concordia Clarke. "I am a senior member of the Council of Conundra!"

Dave ignored her, "The men caught this pair trying to sneak out of the back," he said, succinctly.

I turned to Steve, "Is this them?" I asked.

"Yes," the barman exclaimed, "I'm pretty sure if you hadn't turned up she was going to *drink my blood*! I've been thinking about all this and I reckon I was supposed to be a sacrifice to the dark Lord Cthulhu. Look at that pub sign," he pointed at it, lying on the ground, through the broken door, "Leviathan! If that's a picture of a whale, I'm a monkey's uncle."

I thought once more that I wouldn't want to put Steve on the stand. I had, however, no doubt he'd recognised the pair of them and I couldn't argue with his comment about the pub sign. Deus knows what it was supposed to be.

We were all staring out, trying to decide if it was a whale or an octopus, when a tall figure suddenly appeared in the doorframe: a man in a frock coat with a shock of white hair, a thick moustache and implausibly bushy eyebrows. He was flanked by a group of Celts, some of whom were not blue and looked surprisingly bare as a result. The painted ones were gesturing wildly at the man, who I pegged as the Warlock or at least a Warlock-a-like.

"Murders!" he said to his excited entourage, "Err, no. Calm down! Look, I really can't sort this out for you! Oh Alex, thank goodness you're here," he exclaimed. "Tell them!"

The new arrival rushed free of his group and grabbed at Professor Lidenbrock. Alex patted him reassuringly on the arm.

"Let me introduce Ludovic Bavarian," he said apologetically to us all. "He's an actor."

"But you said you were the Warlock!" complained one of the barefaced Celts to Ludovic. "I thought you were in charge of everything!"

"I hate to break it to you," said Concordia Clarke scathingly, "but Captain Birdseye doesn't actually head up the International Processed Fish Consortium."

Bavarian looked mildly offended at the comparison.

"So he's just one of the Warlock-a-likes?" asked Ray. "Who's the real one?"

"Oh for Pete's sake," said Concordia, "it's obviously Alex. Anyone with half a brain could have spotted that."

We all looked blank

"Let me spell it out: Professor Alex Lidenbrock is the Warlock. He is the secret ruler of Conundra. He set it all up: the money, the social contract, the Hobbesian pact that is his so-called deal. The name of the place is even a sly nod to the Roman name. Who would have done that except a nerd like him?"

I was only moderately surprised. I'd suspected the real Warlock was either Alex or Concordia as soon as I'd met them. As far as I had been able to tell, they were the only people in the city with the requisite confidence. To be honest, I'd been slightly more inclined to think it was Clarke - it seemed in character for her to name the place in honour of herself.

I guessed that, I mouthed at Nemo. He raised his eyebrows in the silent signal of Well, D'uh!

She clearly picked up my thoughts, "But it still occurred to you I might have called the city after myself?" She laughed, "I'd intended to give that impression when I chose 'Concordia' as my nom-de-guerre. The Goddess of social contracts. I could tell it amused the real Warlock. He always enjoys a red herring."

I looked at Alex, who nodded sadly.

"Who else knew you were the Warlock?" I asked him.

"At the start, only Walter West - my original business partner. Then Concordia when I hired her. None of the newer Councilors had any idea."

"Which is a sign of how much attention they're paying. We should sack them all. They're dead weight," Concordia commented.

Alex ignored her, "Then Walter started to get a bit old for all the public appearances, so I hired a team of Warlock look-a-likes to take the load off him, including Ludovic here," he looked appreciatively at the older man. "That worked well. More actors meant the character could feature in a lot more storylines. A guest appearance by the Warlock makes an excellent denouement."

"The ultimate Deus-ex-Machina," said the Warlock-a-like, sweeping into an impressive bow. "A handy way to end any adventure satisfactorily - without having to try too hard."

"Can I just point out," said Ray, "that we'd already resolved everything before you appeared?"

Alex broke in, "Why did you do it Concordia? We had a responsibility towards these people! We had a deal with the subjects of Conundra, for God's sake!"

"Because we were broke!" she hissed. "Your pot of gold ran out three years ago! How did you think I'd been keeping the city running?" She grimaced, "It's not like I wanted to do it. This is my city. We built it from nothing and our greatest duty was to keep it alive! I would do anything that was required. Anything! They weren't our subjects anyway. They were the dregs of Panopticon society. Even they thought so," she pointed at

Nemo and me, "or they would have wanted them in their games!"

Steve stared at me in confusion and I was consumed by guilt. There was a lot for Nemo and me to put right.

"Setting aside for the moment whether it's OK to kill people you don't specifically have a contract with," I said, "what about Katy Potts? She was one of your subjects."

"You killed Katy?" cried Wade, who had remained silent up until then. "But I *knew* her!"

"We'll expect you to confess your part in everything later," Catterwade barked at him and he fell silent and nodded in defeat.

Concordia Clarke had obviously decided there was no point denying anything by this point. Her accomplice Wade was clearly going to rat her out at the slightest pressure from Catterwade or Ray. The fact he was easily bossed around was probably why she'd hired him in the first place.

"I had no choice," said Concordia, "Potts wouldn't let it go. She was about to raise her concerns with the Panopticon. I should never have hired her – she was too new to Conundra and her first loyalty was not to the city. She forced my hand." Concordia looked unrepentant, "I had to give the order to remove her. One of my centurions was following her. He took the required action." She shrugged, "It was unfortunate but necessary."

I turned to Alex Lidenbrock, "If you're actually the Warlock, what happens next is your call. Ray is a Panopticon Undertaker if that helps."

"Actually," commented Ray, "I also passed my Judge exams last month," he paused, "and my Jury qualifications."

"Did you?" I said, surprised. *Judge, jury and executioner?* "Err... Well done?"

"Thanks," he replied, "it's useful in some... special circumstances," he paused, "but the rules are clear: I can't be all three – at least, not in the Panopticon nations. However, this isn't my jurisdiction." He added as an aside for me, "We have no treaties with Conundra covering the legal position of Panopticon Judges or Undertakers."

"Under the Warlock's Deal," stated Alex, "in Conundra, the Warlock and his nominees are entitled to act as judge, jury and executioner."

What a reassuring legal oversight structure, I thought. Especially as it turns out no one actually knew who the Warlock was. A wig, a moustache, and a pair of fake eyebrows appeared to be all you'd need to stage a coup round here. Forget military suppliers, try a joke shop.

It occurred to me that, in practice, Concordia had been the Warlock for years anyway and she knew it. She ran things in the city day-to-day and clearly, in her own mind at least, she was the Council. No coup had been required.

Alex had taken himself out of play by failing to pay attention. If Nemo and I hadn't turned up with our Panopticon tech, he could never have overthrown Concordia and got his throne back. I frowned, it wasn't even clear to me that, under the Warlock's Deal, Concordia had committed any crime. She could argue she was the de-facto Warlock or his nominee, trump up some charges against all the folk she'd murdered, and claim she'd legally passed judgment. I decided to use my own judgment and keep my mouth shut on that. No need to put ideas in anyone's head.

Ray picked up my expression and nodded. We'd need to do something urgently about the appalling

Conundran constitution. I was amazed WorldGov hadn't picked up on it – they were supposed to approve these things. I guessed it must have been waved through after the Summer. To be honest, I wasn't completely happy about Ray's triple qualifications either - even if he never used them together.

Alex continued, "I'm going to leave that cowering Roman senator to you, Ray. He's a Panopticon citizen and he came here to murder another Panopticon citizen. Is that correct?" he addressed Concordia and Wade, who nodded. Alex then turned towards our greasy barman, "And he was about to stab you before Lee arrived?"

Steve seemed about to launch into a long explanation when he caught Ray's eye and just nodded.

"In that case, Ray, he's all yours," said Alex.

Before we went further I had a question for Alex, "Do you have a prison here?"

"We rent some detention space in the Panopticon for that. It's really your area of expertise."

I frowned, "What was Thomas Hobbes' view on the punishment for murder?"

Alex looked grim. "Hobbes and Kant were in complete agreement there."

"An eye for an eye," said Ray.

Alex nodded, "The punishment for murder or attempted murder in Conundra and the Panopticon are the same: death. The Earth no longer has the resources to support humans who won't comply with the fundamental WorldGov laws – we are at war. However," Alex removed his glassed and polished them, "for Kant and Hobbes the punishment wasn't about such practicalities or even deterrents - it was about balance."

Ray walked over to the sobbing senator and looked down at him. "Was this his first specialist excursion here?" he asked Wade.

"He's been here four times," Wade replied.

"We've heard from the witnesses. This is a field trial and I need a jury of three citizens of good standing," said Ray, looking at me, Catterwade and Pip. I knew Nemo's social ranking was too low to serve as a juror for the Panopticon.

"Do you believe this man is guilty?"

I nodded, "We've all done our duty as citizens and reviewed both the content and provenance of the drone feeds from this evening. It's clear the accused man is guilty of attempted murder. The evidence has been confirmed by the intended victim." I spoke clearly for the benefit of the streamed Panopticon audience.

I wondered if this was an unusually clear-cut case or if we always had so much video footage there were never any miscarriages of justice in the Panopticon. I felt uncomfortable - that couldn't be true unless all jurors were adept users of tech and able to carefully verify data. I knew from personal experience they weren't. I resolved to ask Laura to run over the Judge and Jury exam papers with me - I'd give the Undertaker exams a miss for now.

"In that case," said Ray, "I find the accused guilty of the attempted murder of Steve Johnson, a Panopticon citizen. Due to lack of recorded evidence I cannot pass judgment on any previous crimes. The sentence for attempted murder is death. I confirm I am qualified by WorldGov to pass such a Judgement and separately qualified to execute on it." Ray took his gun out of his holster.

The senator looked up, suddenly paying attention to what was going on around him. "No, wait," he said, "I'm sorry I killed them! It was just a holiday!" he shrieked. "I'm only a tourist!"

Ray shot him in the forehead.

"You know what I hate?" he said. "Tourists," and re-holstered his weapon.

"Justice is quick in the Panopticon," I murmured. We had all seen too many deaths since '36 to shed any tears for the senator. With the data we had, the Panopticon citizenry expected swift action in full public view.

"'He that is taken and put into prison or chains is not conquered, though overcome; for he is still an enemy' – Thomas Hobbes," said Alex.

"But what happens in Conundra, stays in Conundra," whispered Wade.

"Not anymore," said Alex, shifting his attention to Concordia.

"This is not a Panopticon state. This Judge has no jurisdiction here!" she shouted. "This is my city. I had every right to protect it – I was the Warlock really! Alex! I'm your friend! You can't let them kill me!" she demanded. "I had to do it. Since the money ran out we couldn't keep this place going. You asked me to find a way! People will pay so much for our special services – you wouldn't believe how profitable they are! What choice did I have?"

"I thought you'd cut the bloody hospitality budget!" Alex yelled. "We could have worked something out! You knew I would never have agreed to what you did!"

"That's because you're too weak to rule this city!" Concordia retorted. "Cheaper handwash was hardly going to save Conundra! Someone needed to take radical action or the city would have collapsed! I was the only one with the strength of will! If a few fools like this idiot bartender had to be sacrificed – so be it."

The Warlock straightened his spine and looked gravely at Ray, who handed him his revolver and nodded. "Then we should have let Conundra fall," Alex said gravely and shot her.

AUREUS

Conundra, September 2054

Later that night, as we all sat drinking Steve's beer, Alex told me that in 2036 he'd been an archeology student at the local university. When the firestorm hit, he'd just made it into an emergency shelter in the basement of a concrete college building. For 24 hours he'd been crammed in with his classmates and a few town folk, including some who'd been staging a play in the local theatre.

The city was caught by a huge, freak wall of flame that swept along the east coast. When Alex and his companions emerged from the shelter the world looked like it had been carpet-bombed.

Most of the surviving inhabitants joined the refugee trail to London but Alex stayed behind with a few of the others to help clear the debris.

"I spent six months sharing a tent with an ageing actor called Walter West. Our job was tidy up. We shifted tons of masonry - cleared everything down to the ground. In the evenings, we talked about how we'd rebuild everything - of course, we never thought we'd really get the chance."

Ah, I thought, so this was how they met.

"In a couple of places, Walter and I cleared all the way down to the layer of ash from the previous time the place was burned - by Boudicca." He mused, "When I was a kid, I'd been obsessed with the Fenwick hoard - the idea treasure might be buried anywhere under the city just waiting to be found."

"I was amazed the hoard survived the Summer," I said.

"Everything important was sent to the British Museum for safe keeping at the start of '36." Alex sighed, "It was a hell of a job to persuade them to give it back."

I asked, "So, what did you and Walter find?"

"Without my old metal detector, the answer probably would've been nothing. It's a measure of how far I thought civilization had collapsed that I used one at all. I was supposed to be an archaeologist - not a tomb raider," he grimaced, "but back then it didn't feel like genteel digging at ruins was ever likely to happen again."

I nodded.

"We found what I'd always dreamed of." He stared off into space for a moment, "Gold. Gold and silver and copper coins. Crates of the stuff. All below the Roman ash layer. Buried before Boudicca's army arrived, just like the Fenwick hoard. Only, this wasn't a few pieces of jewellery. This was more money than you've ever seen. So much! Over the years we found eight more caches but the biggest was the first. Of course, we'd never have found any of them if the place hadn't been razed."

"Where the hell did it all come from?" I asked.

"Seneca and his friends. I told you, lenders flooded Britain with money after the Roman invasion then panicked and called it all in – they got scared Nero was going to pull out of the province. It was their run on Britain that really sparked the Celtic rebellion. A lot of the cash extracted from the locals came through Camulodunum. Obviously, the citizens hid it before Boudicca arrived. I always wondered if that was why the Celts took so long to get to Londinium – maybe they were searching the ruins of this city for the money."

"But they didn't have metal detectors."

Alex shook his head. "They probably tortured people to try to find the caches, but that's somewhat less effective," he added, dryly. "No one in this story is a hero."

"So, you found a treasure load of solid gold coins, just when all the world's currencies were failing. No wonder you bought yourself a small country."

"Gold and silver were worth an incredible amount then. We'd spent the whole first cache by 2038. I managed to get all the land rights assigned to me and recognised by WorldGov quite quickly – in '37 bullion could buy you anything you wanted. We used the coins to form the state, pay for food and shelter for our workforce, and rebuild the centre.

We couldn't exchange the coins for money – we just had to spend it as barter before anyone noticed and took it off us. Loads of people were using jewellery as currency back then so as long as we were careful, we didn't stand out. Our plan was to convert the coins into a physical city – walls, buildings and subjects.

We invented the Warlock character and Walter agreed to play him – he bleached his hair whiter to start with and grew a bigger moustache so people wouldn't recognise him. I preferred to run things from behind the scenes. Legally, of course, it was all in my name."

"When did you run out of coins?" I asked.

"We found the last cache five years ago. We spent that in two years."

"I'm surprised you didn't sell the Fenwick hoard," I remarked.

Alex winced.

"Ah," I said, "you did."

"Eighteen months ago," he said, wryly. "All the stuff in the museum is fake. Then Concordia told me she'd sorted everything out. The books balanced – I thought she'd just made the stories cheaper. Dammit! I was such a naive idiot. This is all my fault!"

AFTERMATH

Conundra, September
2054

The next afternoon, we all gathered in the Warlock's office in the Council building on Rubicon Road. Alex had moved in there and publically assumed the title of Warlock. He had decided to run things directly himself. There was a white wig, moustache and a pair of fake eyebrows lying on his desk.

"I have to wear them for official business," he remarked. "We'll keep Ludovic and the other actors to play the Warlock in our storylines, otherwise I'll never get anything done – the character is too valuable to lose."

I looked out of the huge windows at the city. It felt like it should be in flames after our battle the previous night, but everything looked exactly as before. The city would happily continue without Concordia Clarke and Wade Scarlett.

I'd spent much of the morning being thoroughly confessed to by Wade. He had decided to tell us everything in order to avoid the abrupt end of his boss. We now knew Concordia had been running the snuff minibreaks for nearly two years. Just a handful at first, while she perfected things, but getting increasingly frequent in the last few months. It sounded like murder was becoming a production line in Conundra. Wade had given us the details of the previous snuffbreak purchasers, all from the Panopticon, and arrests were in progress by the relevant state police.

Ray and Alex had agreed Wade wouldn't share Concordia's fate. One of the changes we needed to bring about in society was to stop citizens, or subjects, from blindly following orders no matter how illegal or unethical. Unfortunately, that was still a work in progress.

Wade was one of those people who did what they were told. If we executed all of them, our psychologists told us, there would only be about 20% of humanity left. No, we decided, Wade was fit and healthy. He and Concordia's centurion thugs would join the Panopticon prison work gangs. They would dig irrigation trenches in Devon, where work was behind schedule. Everyone in the Panopticon would know what they'd done – they would be closely watched for the rest of their lives.

After I'd left Wade signing a confession I had dropped in on Steve Johnson at the Leviathan bar. He looked showered and was dressed in tweed trousers and a clean linen shirt. His sleeves were rolled up and he was sweeping the floors.

The formerly-greasy barman put down his broom for a moment and informed me he'd decided to stay in Conundra. The Warlock had asked him to take over as the new Leviathan manager and there was a flat above he could live in.

I was curious if he would miss the Panopticon and he thought about it for a moment, "You know, I never really felt like the Panopticon wanted me." He leaned on his new bar and said that was why he'd followed Concordia when she had offered to pay off his debts and give me a job somewhere new – a clean slate.

"It seemed too good to be true even at the time," he admitted, "but what did I have to lose?"

Finally, I'd phoned Dave in the Celtic camp to check on the state of his army. He told me everyone was hungover and had decided it was their best holiday ever. Apparently, they weren't the only ones. Since the battle had gone out on the Panopticon feeds, the Conundra bookings team had been overrun with orders for Celts v Romans packages. After lunch, walking up the stairs to Alex's new office, I'd passed a line of would-be Boudiccas queuing to audition for a role in their new blockbuster storyline.

♦ ♦ ♦

"'The source of every crime, is some defect of the understanding; or some error in reasoning; or some sudden force of the passions'," quoted Alex grimly as we all sat together that afternoon, "Thomas Hobbes."

"Don't feel bad about Concordia," said Ray, "'I had a budget to balance' is not a legal defense. I should know - I'm a judge, jury and executioner."

"The trouble is, she was right," continued Alex, "we just don't have enough money coming in.

Without Concordia's snuff minibreak income the city will collapse inside six months."

"Actually," I interrupted, "I'll buy Conundra."

BEHEMOTH

*Conundra, September
2054*

N emo grinned and Alex looked at me as if I was crazy.

It wasn't a bad business plan. Deciding whether I wanted to buy the place was the real reason I'd come to Conundra - holidays were never my scene. Nemo and I had known for ages we needed to hire a creative team to help us manage our sim storylines and keep everything running smoothly. From what I'd seen here, we could build on the existing Conundra staff - in the real world they were already doing what we needed in our virtual Worlds.

I'd looked at the city's accounts last night. With the receipts from Concordia's secret snuff conspiracy the place had been doing OK. The irony was, I didn't think she'd needed to offer anything so murdery.

I guessed, being an ex-horror director, it was the first money-spinning plan that came into her head. Perhaps she'd always liked the idea and was just looking for an excuse. There was, however, plenty of other stuff that was legal under WorldGov but generally disapproved of in the Panopticon states. Those activities were ripe for a themed vacation away from the all-seeing-eye and they were 100% legit. The WorldGov laws were remarkably liberal – it was only the Panopticon citizenry who weren't. As long as you didn't kill anyone, World President Gates was fairly relaxed about how you spent your free time.

Under Nemo's and my ownership, Conundra could return vice to the average Panopticon citizen. We'd not buy Alex out completely – we needed him to run things and he could keep all his historical reenactment storylines – there was a perfectly good market for that. I'd love to add something futuristic too because everyone likes speculative fiction. It would have to be cheap though – probably post-apocalyptic.

"Concordia Clarke clearly guessed I was here as a potential buyer," I said to the stunned Alex. "She wouldn't have given me the treatment she did otherwise – she probably would've shot me. In her defense, she did find a solution to your money problems – it was just a bad one. There were other paths she could have taken."

My brother chipped in, "Vice. We reckon we could make a lot of money. We would do everything within WorldGov laws. No one would get hurt and it'd be more lucrative than going round stabbing people."

"And less, err, evil," I added. "There's plenty of sex and drugs goes on in places like Edge City, but only for folk who've given up on social acceptability." I glanced at my brother, who looked smug. "Of course, eyes on it keep it policed, which is not a bad thing. You'd need oversight here too. You could use the Gothic zone as the location: it's run down – needs a cash injection – but it's well positioned for a red light district."

I wondered what would've happened if I hadn't run across the murder of Katy Potts and innocently bankrolled Conundra. I'd probably have set up a Vice sector with Concordia Clarke. I reckoned she'd have been good at it too.

If she'd had a legal revenue stream, would she have stopped bumping people off? I suspected not. According to Hercule Poirot, killing people was a Rubicon - once you started, you kept at it.

Anyway, I thought, *Nemo, Pip and the Panopticon were already onto her scheme. They would have found Concordia out eventually.* It was hard to commit crimes any more. The only reason her spree went on as long as it did was because things could still be hidden in Conundra. Moving back and forth between the city and the Panopticon was especially dangerous. It was too easy for people to disappear.

That reminded me, "If we're going to do this," I said, "we need some new treaties between the Panopticon and Conundra. We should at least put Panopticon cameras in the Conundran farms and factories so the city can get the Seal for exports."

"Plus," said Alex, "we need some cross-border rules on ratings for my subjects. It's hard for them to visit the Panopticon states because they don't have any social scores there. It's also difficult for your citizens to come here for more than a few weeks - the blank area it leaves in their recorded history counts against them. Unsynced social credit scores mean that, in reality, we don't have free movement of people."

"And there should be proper records, so people can't go missing between the states any more. And we'll want some access to the Conundran cameras for shared policing." added Pip.

"I think we're going to need to set up a Panopticon embassy here and start negotiations." I stated.

♦ ♦ ♦

Eventually, the others left. Pip Marlowe went to tidy up her grubby office now it was officially, if temporarily, the local embassy of the Panopticon Nations.

Alex poured us both a Scotch.

"To our business partnership," he said.

"We've got plenty to do," I replied, clinking my glass to his, "You know, that stuff about harmonizing social scores is going to be harder than you think. Ratings are not set by the

Panopticon - they're the domain of Omniscience Industries and Kirby Cross. He's not going to like the idea of people being invisible to the all-seeing-eye without taking a social hit."

"I have some ideas." Alex smiled, "We could have our own private rating system here - set by the Council. All we'd have to do is agree a way of mapping it to Kirby's scores. Our subjects could share their Conundra score with Omniscience if they want. I suspect Kirby's algorithms currently assume this place is all sex'n'drugs..."

"...when, in reality, it's mostly treasure hunts and ice lollies," I finished, nodding my head. Conundra was surprisingly clean-cut right now - apart from the grisly murders, of course.

A mapped social score wasn't a bad idea. If it was managed well and it was clear how the scoring worked then Kirby would probably go for it. I was glad Alex was stepping up and becoming the Warlock again.

"I'm thinking of calling it the Leviathan score," he said.

The Leviathan Score. I approved. It sounded like a trashy thriller.

"I want to be constantly reminded of Katy Potts and of everyone else Concordia murdered – of how many deaths I caused by not paying attention," Alex continued, running his hand through his hair.

Wade had told us they'd killed seventeen people with the snuff minibreak scheme. We were lucky it wasn't more – they'd only just started scaling up the process.

"You didn't kill them," I said, gently.

"No, but they were my responsibility. The Warlock's Deal is very clear. They gave up their right to look out for each other by coming here. In exchange, my promise was to act wisely and keep them safe. I delegated that to Concordia and it was a terrible mistake. Sovereign authority is only a good thing if it is competent enough to execute on its contracts. Hobbes called a government that had lost control a Behemoth: 'The obligation of subjects to the sovereign is understood to last as long, and no longer, than the power lasteth by which he is able to protect them'."

I pondered that for a second. Leviathan vs Behemoth: a giant sea creature versus a lumbering land one. Sounded like a Japanese monster movie.

Maybe Hobbes had missed a trick and we needed something more amphibious. I wondered what a Godzilla government would look like. Mostly asleep, but occasionally it wakes up to stomp everything flat? On the plus side, that would force you to regularly rethink things. On the negative side, it could be messy.

I shook my head. *Concentrate Lee.*

"Isn't that a common problem with rule by a single authority?" I replied, "Concordia Clarke got away with anything she liked. She was completely unaccountable."

"She was supposed to be accountable to me – if I'd been doing my job properly as sovereign."

"But who were you accountable to?"

"That's why I have something to ask you," Alex continued, "I need to reorganise this place – encourage the police to be more than a bumbling sideshow, set up some checks and balances."

And re-write the Warlock's Deal as a proper constitution. And sort out a succession system, I thought.

"Would you stay here and help me re-found Conundra? Make it right this time?"

I paused in shock.

I liked Alex and he'd accomplished something amazing: the only stable state in the world outside the Panopticon. I loved the Conundra concept and their creative teams would really help Nemo and me with our games. The city could also be a great earner - I had plenty of ideas already - but live here? In my opinion, having a sovereign and being a subject were kind of infantilizing.

Conundra was a fun holiday but you couldn't live this way all the time. The point of the Panopticon, and what I respected about it, was it was the antithesis of escapism - the opposite of Conundra. In the Panopticon nations, you were always fully informed. Sometimes brutally so. It was hard, but it was *real.*

I saw that having somewhere to occasionally take a few days off from the raw truth was useful, but I couldn't understand why anyone would become a full-time Conundran subject. To achieve your potential, I reckoned, you had to live in the world as it was not kid yourself about the truth. It was like Kant said – complete disclosure was a necessary part of being fully human.

Alex was staring at me hopefully. *He doesn't need my help*, I thought. He set this place up and he was more than capable of finding a new Head of Mystery and Intrigue and getting the constitution sorted out.

The cash injection Nemo and I had handed over would give him plenty of time to fix things. The Panopticon was keen to help – anything to get better eyes on this place as far as they were concerned – and Ray and Nemo were happy to stick around for a while. They'd both gone out that morning to shop for togas. Alex had everything he needed except a new Walter West and I didn't want to wear that particular fake moustache.

"Why did you set Conundra up the way you did? As escapism?" I asked, playing for time.

Alex laughed, "For the reasons you'd guess. I was a huge game player before the Summer. Dungeons and Dragons, Call of Cthulhu – everything really – and there were loads of post-apocalyptic live action role-players who'd escaped the Summer and had useful skills for the new world. A lot of them signed up to be my first subjects."

I loved role-playing too, but I wasn't sure I wanted it to be my entire existence. I was desperately trying to think of a nice way to tell Alex I thought he was living in a theme park, when the phone on his desk rang and he picked it up.

"It's for you," he passed me the handset. "Someone from the Panopticon Assembly?"

I grabbed the phone in relief, wondering what could be so urgent they needed to call me here.

"Lee?" I recognised Laura. "Thank goodness!" her voice sounded strained. "We've had a distress call from the Moon. WorldGov needs you to go there right away."

"Me?" I said, incredulously, "Why on Earth would WorldGov want me on the Moon? I know absolutely nothing about the space program. What could I possibly help with?"

"There's been a murder on one of the bases," replied Laura.

I still didn't know why I'd be useful.

"The killer was from one of your Worlds. It was a denizen," she paused, "and it has escaped."

EPILOGUE

Utopia Six: Pre-Launch Version 378

The schoolhouse reformed itself in front of me and the tornado reversed its way back through the burning forest, the funnel's flames extinguishing themselves.

I needed to follow the twister back to the moment of formation. Why hadn't the Samara devices removed enough energy to dissipate it? Were we not spotting the storm early enough?

Nemo appeared beside me, wearing a toga. "Where's your space suit?" he said. "Aren't you supposed to be taking off today?"

"I'm in the rocket now but there's a lot of sitting around on the pad waiting for launch. I thought I'd get something actually useful done."

"More useful than catching a murderous denizen loose on the Moon?"

"Yeah," I sighed in annoyance. "We both know that'll be a load of crap. Everyone anthropomorphizes the denizens."

"Never ascribe to the spontaneous appearance of general artificial intelligence, that which could be explained by incompetence," said Nemo. "Sand's Law of Robotics."

"Absolutely. How is a chatbot going to murder anyone? They'll have done something idiotic like hooked it up to an airlock door and then made some comment about the place being stuffy." I frowned, "My guess is, I'll have the whole thing sorted out inside an hour. What a waste of time! I bet I could have handled it remotely if WorldGov weren't being so bloody secretive."

"You're grumpy for the one about to be launched into space," commented my brother, resentfully.

"I guess I still feel like shit about those people we just got killed."

"Was it really our fault?" he asked. "We hardly designed the feature with psycho murderers in mind. Concordia Clarke could have just stuck a pin in a phone book to pick her victims."

"Using our loser list gave her a way better result than that."

"True, but she could have found some other way to choose them. If we made vans and she used one of them to run over her victims, would that make it our fault? It wouldn't have been what we designed the vans for. Unless we put bull bars on, of course."

"I know what you're saying," I replied, "but I wonder if we were more responsible than that. I keep thinking about Kant and treating people like means or ends. When we picked the people to not looks-upgrade we didn't consider the effect it might have on them. Anyone who saw them in our Worlds knew we thought they were losers. They must have felt it because *everyone* plays our stuff. I keep wondering if that was why Steve agreed to go with Concordia - that maybe we forced him out of the Panopticon."

"We only tagged them as losers because they already were." Nemo looked thoughtful, "Although I'll admit we didn't help. In fact, we probably did make the situation worse." He shrugged, "You don't upgrade your looks in the games either and no one tries to murder you... err...that often."

It was a good point. I didn't take the attractiveness upgrade in our games because it ate into my denizens' cpu allocations – I'd rather the VR versions of me were smarter and faster than better looking – but the real me was rich enough to not care what other people thought.

There was another thing worrying me though. We'd only started investigating the disappearances because we reckoned all those people couldn't have emigrated out of the Panopticon willingly – but they all had. They'd planned to live in Conundra and never return. That Concordia Clarke didn't genuinely intend to take them in didn't change the fact those people had wanted to leave the Panopticon and were willing to take a dodgy-sounding deal to do it. That concerned me.

"How are things in our game worlds, now everyone gets the looks-upgrade?" I asked.

"Oh," said Nemo, "it worked out fine. As soon as the stigma went out of not being airbrushed, loads of players decided to opt-out. They wanted the extra processing speed - just like you." He smirked, "Your denizens won't have the game advantages they used to anymore."

I didn't know what Nemo was looking so smug about. It was him who tweaked my denizens' luck to keep them alive. If they had fewer advantages, that would be more work for him, not me. I smirked back.

"Do you reckon Kirby Cross is a warlord?" I asked, changing the subject. "Is World President Gates? The Earth *is* fairly authoritarian by pre-Summer standards."

"You don't usually worry about that stuff."

"I couldn't help noticing Conundra displayed all the classic problems of the benign dictatorship."

My brother nodded, "You start out with Professor Alex, tweed suits and elbow patches. A decade later it's Concordia Clarke and her centurion death squads?"

"Indeed.   The thing about being a benign dictator is you actually have to be benign. And the succession planning often seems to leave something to be desired."

"You're worried we're living in a fool's paradise? With Kirby and Gates in charge, everything's fine right now but what about the next warlord – or warlady of course?" said Nemo.

"Warperson? Yes, I am a little worried by the successions," I replied.

"Join the club. By the way, why did you really decide to buy Conundra? It's a risky decision for you." He grinned, "The whole place will be underwater in a few years anyway."

A countdown broke into the simulation. "Sounds like we're taking off, I'd better pay attention – this will be my only go at this."

I switched back to the real world view out of my visor and gazed at the other passengers. I was in two minds about this Moon trip. Legally, it was a grey area whether I should have been allowed off-planet. Space was limited to specialists and I didn't have the qualifying skillset. *WorldGov must really be panicking over this denizen thing.* I thought.

As the countdown hit "One!" I thought about Nemo's final question. Why had I bought Conundra? I smiled to myself. That was easy. A place that had recreated itself once could do it again – or as many times as needed to survive. Plus, it had been a fun holiday.

Maybe one day I'd take another.

TIMELINE

0043   – The Roman Conquest of Britain.

0061   – The Iceni Rebellion, Boudicca burns Camulodunum and Londinium.

2025   – 8th January 2025 is Full Transparency Day. The day the Panopticon is turned on.

2030   – Deus1 launches.

'30-'35 – The Panopticon is gradually rolled out worldwide accompanied by a reduction in crime, more informed debate, better political engagement, and higher productivity. Deus builds on its lead and becomes the most widely used and trusted application in the world.

2036   – The Hot Summer: fires, floods, ice storms, and tornados engulf the globe. Over one billion are killed. Mass exoduses occur from many land masses and areas. The refugee population surges. Colchester is burned to the ground.

2037   – WorldGov and the Panopticon Assemblies are formed.

2037   – Stillsuits invented.

2037   – City of Conundra is formed.

2038   – The Quantum Leap occurs – vastly improved image processing and storage using quantum technology.

2040   – Nautilus 1: Sauron's Eye. The first full world-sim based on Panopticon data is launched (will become Control).

2043   – Dystopia 1 launches.

2045   – DeusX launches.

2053   – Utopia Five launches.

2054   – Lee Sands visits Conundra.

Printed in Poland
by Amazon Fulfillment
Poland Sp. z o.o., Wrocław